HAINTS
OF THE HILLS

HAINTS
OF THE HILLS

DANIEL W. BAREFOOT

JOHN F. BLAIR, PUBLISHER
WINSTON-SALEM, NORTH CAROLINA

Published by John F. Blair, Publisher

The paper in this book meets the guidelines
for permanence and durability of the
Committee on Production Guidelines

Cover photograph of Black Mountains courtesy of
North Carolina Division of Tourism, Film and Sports Development
Map courtesy of
North Carolina Department of Transportation
Design by Debra Long Hampton

Library of Congress Cataloging-in-Publication Data

Barefoot, Daniel W., 1951–
Haints of the hills / Daniel W. Barefoot.
p.   cm.—(North Carolina's haunted hundred ; v. 3)
ISBN 0-89587-259-5
1. Ghosts—North Carolina. 2. Haunted places—North Carolina.
3. Apparitions—North Carolina. I. Title.
BF1472.U6 B363 2002
133.1'09756'8—dc21
2002003358

To my dear mother,
Ramona P. Barefoot, who gave me
the family roots in the North Carolina mountains

CONTENTS

PREFACE

*Once upon a midnight dreary, while I pondered, weak and
   weary
Over many a quaint and curious volume of forgotten lore,
While I nodded, nearly napping, suddenly there came a
   tapping,
As of some one gently rapping . . .*

Edgar Allan Poe

In my hometown of Lincolnton, the western horizon is domi-
nated by the majestic North Carolina mountains. These beautiful
mountains, the tallest and oldest in all of eastern America, ex-
cite the imagination of all who look upon them. They have long
provided a source of inspiration for writers, artists, and roman-
tics. In the hills of North Carolina, the imagination is free to
wander. But truth is stranger than fiction. Indeed, the supernatural
beings and events of the North Carolina mountains are some of
the most bizarre in the annals of American folklore.

As a child growing up in North Carolina in the 1950s
and 1960s, I delighted in watching Rod Serling's *The Twilight
Zone* television series and the great science-fiction films of

that period. At the same time, I read with great interest the classic ghost stories of North Carolina, as documented by John Harden in *The Devil's Tramping Ground* (1949) and *Tar Heel Ghosts* (1954) and by Nancy Roberts in *An Illustrated Guide to Ghosts & Other Mysterious Occurrences in the Old North State* (1959) and *Ghosts of the Carolinas* (1962).

Meanwhile, I was developing an abiding interest in the magnificent history of North Carolina. The history of the state—indeed, the history of British America—began on the soil of North Carolina with Sir Walter Raleigh's colonization attempts, which resulted in the Lost Colony of Roanoke in the 1580s. Ironically, our history as Tar Heels began with a haunting mystery that remains unresolved to this day.

When the European traditions of ghosts, witches, demons, and the like were brought to America, they landed on the shores of North Carolina. And it was on our soil that settlers documented some of the first encounters with the supernatural in America. But long before the arrival of European settlers, North Carolina was the domain of various Indian peoples. Theirs is a history replete with tales of the supernatural.

Because North Carolina has been a significant part of the American experience from the very beginning, it has emerged as one of the most historic places in the United States. And where there is history, ghosts and other elements of the supernatural can usually be found. As a longtime student of the Old North State, I can assure readers that North Carolina has a haunted heritage, one rich in the supernatural.

This book and its companion volumes offer a view of that ghostly history in a format never before presented. Here, for the first time, readers are offered a supernatural tale from each of the state's one hundred counties. But the *North Carolina's Haunted Hundred* series is not simply a collection of Tar Heel ghost stories from every county in the state. Rather, it is a sampler of the diverse supernatural history of North Carolina. The three volumes contain accounts of ghosts and apparitions (human, animal, and inanimate), witches, strange creatures, demons, spook lights, haunting mysteries, unidentified flying objects, unexplained phenomena, and more.

Instead of retelling the timeless ghost stories so well chronicled by Harden, Roberts, Fred T. Morgan, F. Roy Johnson, Judge Charles Harry Whedbee, and others, I have chosen to present many tales that have never been widely circulated in print. I include a few of the familiar tales of our ghostly lore in the mix, but with new information or a new twist.

Do you believe in ghosts and creatures of the night? Whether your answer is yes or no, almost everyone enjoys a ghost story or an inexplicable tale of the unusual. And when that narrative has as its basis real people, actual places, and recorded events, it becomes more enjoyable because it hints at credibility and believability.

All of the stories set forth in this three-volume series are based in fact. But over the years, these tales have been told and retold, and the details have in some cases become blurred. As with all folklore, whether you choose to believe any or all of the accounts in these pages is entirely up to you. A caveat that Mark Twain once offered his readers holds true here: "I will set down a tale. . . . It may be only a legend, a tradition. It may have happened, it may not have happened. But it could have happened."

Should you develop a desire to visit some of the haunted places detailed in this series, be mindful that most are located on private property. Be sure to obtain permission from the owner before attempting to go upon any site.

The seemingly endless peaks, ridges, valleys, and coves of the North Carolina mountains offer a panorama of natural beauty unexcelled anywhere on earth. These hills and vales also contain a plethora of supernatural beings—some evil, others simply mysterious, but all captivating. In the pages that follow, these haints of the hills are sure to entertain you or chill your bones.

ACKNOWLEDGMENTS

Writing a three-volume work with subject matter from each
of the one hundred counties of North Carolina has given me a
much deeper appreciation for the vastness of the state. To complete a project of this size and scope, I needed the assistance and
kindly offices of innumerable people and many institutions. To
all of them, I am truly grateful. There are, however, individuals
who deserve special mention for their efforts on my behalf.

Extensive research was essential for the successful completion of this project. Librarians and their assistants at numerous
county and municipal libraries throughout the state helped in
that task by searching for materials, offering advice, and extend-
ing other courtesies to me. Pat Harden of the Norris Public Library in Rutherfordton; Chris Bates, the curator of the Carolina
Room at the Public Library of Charlotte-Mecklenburg County;
and Fred Turner of the Olivia Raney Local History Library in
Raleigh were particularly helpful. At the reference section in the
State Library of North Carolina and in the search room of the
North Carolina State Archives, I always received prompt and
courteous attention and assistance. At the University of North
Carolina at Chapel Hill, Bob Anthony and his staff at the North

Carolina Collection and the staff at the Southern Historical Collection rendered the same outstanding assistance as they did on my prior books. At other academic libraries in the state, including those at Duke University, East Carolina University, and Appalachian State University, the special-collections personnel helped to point me in the right direction in my quest for information.

This project represents the fifth time around for me in working with Carolyn Sakowski and the excellent staff at John F. Blair, Publisher. Carolyn saw the merit in my proposal from the outset, and she was instrumental in its evolution into a three-book set. As in each of my past efforts, Steve Kirk has gone beyond the call of duty to provide his expertise as my editor. His patience, good and timely advice, keen insight, and knowledge of many subjects are deeply appreciated, and his hard work has added immeasurably to the quality of this book. Debbie Hampton, Anne Waters, Ed Southern, and all of the others at Blair are a pleasure to work with in production, publicity, and marketing.

When I issued a request for "good" ghost stories, my colleagues in the North Carolina General Assembly came to the aid of the person they refer to as their "resident historian." Special assistance was provided by Representative Bill Hurley of Fayetteville, Representative Phil Haire of Sylva, Representative Wayne Goodwin of Hamlet, and Representative Leslie Cox of Sanford.

Friends from far and wide provided support for my efforts. At the University of North Carolina at Wilmington, my friend and fellow author Dr. Chris Fonvielle offered advice and encouragement. In my hometown of Lincolnton, my friends often greeted me with a common question: "What are you writing now, Dan?" When I responded with details about *North Carolina's Haunted Hundred*, they were universally enthusiastic about the series. My crosstown friend, George Fawcett, considered by many to be the foremost authority on unidentified flying objects in North Carolina, welcomed the opportunity to provide from his vast files materials on a credible UFO landing on Tar Heel soil. Darrell Harkey, the Lincoln County historical coordinator, provided words of encouragement and friendship when they were needed most.

For its unending assistance, support, and love, I owe my family an enormous debt of gratitude I can never repay. Because of my family roots, I hold a close kinship with each of the three geographic regions in the *Haunted Hundred* set. In the 1920s, my paternal grandparents left their home in Columbus County on the coast to settle in Gaston County. About the same time, my maternal grandparents left their home in western North Carolina to put down roots in Gaston. In that Piedmont county, east thus met west, and my parents married and reared a son there.

My late father introduced me to the intriguing world of ghosts and the supernatural by taking me to those now-campy horror films of the late fifties and early sixties. My mother taught me the love of reading and writing at an early age. Both parents instilled in me a love of my native state.

My sister remains an ardent supporter of my career as a writer and historian.

My daughter, Kristie, has literally grown up while I have written eight books over the past seven years. With forbearance and love, she has endured the travels and travails of a father who has attempted to balance a career in law, politics, and history with a normal family life. Now a junior at the University of North Carolina at Chapel Hill, she has somehow found time in her extremely busy schedule to type portions of my hand-written manuscripts.

No one deserves more praise and credit for this book and all my others than my wife and best friend, Kay. It was Kay who encouraged me to combine my interests in North Carolina history and the supernatural heritage of our state to produce this book and its companion volumes. As with my previous books, Kay has meticulously read and reread every word and has acted as my sounding board for sentence structure and vocabulary. But more than that, her smiling face, her praise for me even when it's not merited, her willingness to support my every endeavor and to proudly stand beside me, her genuine kindness and unique grace, and her boundless love and constant companionship for more than twenty-seven years have blessed my life with a measure of happiness that few men ever have the good fortune to enjoy.

HAINTS
OF THE HILLS

DIAMOND JIM'S MANSION

None remain but a few ghosts
Of timorous heart, to linger on.

Robert Graves

HIDDENITE, a small community in east-central Alexander County, has been known as a gem town since William Earl Hidden, a New York mineralogist and an associate of Thomas Edison, arrived here in 1880 and discovered a gem found nowhere else in the world. He named his rare treasure hiddenite, and the town promptly changed its name from White Plains.

In the years since Hidden's famous discovery, numerous gem mines have operated at various times in and around Hiddenite. In the late twentieth century, the village yielded the world's largest emerald. The most tangible evidence of the wealth this village has produced is the former Lucas Mansion, located on SR 1001 just north of its intersection with NC 90 in the heart of Hiddenite. Strangely enough, the opulence of the rambling, three-story, twenty-two-room Victorian mansion did not come from the gems of Hiddenite, but rather from diamonds. The fascinating story behind this house is one of mystery and ghosts.

When the original portion of the house was constructed around 1900, it did not in any way resemble the large, over-stated mansion that survives today. A young couple, Richard and Margaret, built a small, two-story wooden cottage in anticipation of their marriage. Richard was not a favorite of the local old-timers, who yet remembered the hardships of the War Between the States. To them, he was nothing more than a contemptible "damn Yankee" who had come to the South and stolen the heart of a lovely, innocent local girl.

As it turned out, the lingering animosities over the war ended the wedding dreams of Richard and Margaret. One day, the two were sitting on a boulder near the cottage they were to share when Richard launched into a stern, impassioned soliloquy: "You must make up your mind, commit yourself to me, live as I believe, admit that the Civil War was fought to preserve the union. Lincoln did not hate the South. Jefferson Davis is a traitor. Stoneman was my good friend; he was loyal to what it took to impoverish the South, to bring it to its knees. You can't go back to your petty aristocracy, to your ruffled umbrellas and pointed shoes. This shall be our reconstruction for the South, you and I in the little honeymoon cottage I built for us, the Union and the Confederate to bring about a new order. Margaret, I love you, my beautiful, brilliant, refined girl. What is your answer?"

With fire in her eyes and venom in her voice, the usually sweet, demure young woman shot back a quick retort: "If you expect me to accept you on those terms, your brains must be a mess of scrambled eggs!"

Richard was unyielding. "I'm leaving," he said. "I will dispose of the honeymoon cottage. It was full of love and hope of our lives together. I leave you to your world of yesterday, and I will leave our house of dreams. My tender love built its walls.

You will forget that I ever lived. Seethe in your hatred of Lincoln, Sherman, and Stoneman!"

Exit Richard and Margaret and enter James Paul Lucas (1878-1952), who began a lifelong love affair with Hiddenite as a boy when he attended a boarding school in the area. As a young man, Lucas became an extremely successful salesman and importer of diamonds. "Diamond Jim," as he was known, eventually retired as general manager of Samstag and Hilder Brothers, a famous gemstone firm in New York City.

In the course of his work, Diamond Jim attained great wealth. He moved his parents, J. F. and Sally Lucas, into the would-be honeymoon cottage at Hiddenite in the first decade of the twentieth century. His father had served as a bugler for General Robert E. Lee during the War Between the States and had played a tune for Generals Lee and Grant at the famous surrender at Appomattox.

From 1915 to 1920, Diamond Jim transformed the cottage into a mansion by making the second story into a third story and adding a new second story. He also added a sweeping veranda. He equipped his summer castle with modern conveniences unheard of in the area. A power plant on the grounds provided electricity. A hydraulic pumping system delivered running water to all three floors.

Diamond Jim furnished his mansion in grand style with prized pieces from around the world. Displayed throughout the house were one-of-a-kind items: a smoking pipe once owned by Czar Nicholas of Russia; nautical instruments from the flagship of Admiral Dewey; clothing of Buffalo Bill; chaps worn by Will Rogers; boxing gloves used by John L. Sullivan and James J. Corbett; Pancho Villa's sombrero; and countless gifts from noted statesmen, actors, and other notable persons. His collection of 150 clocks scattered throughout the house created a din that few visitors ever forgot.

By the time he retired to the mansion at Hiddenite in 1928, Diamond Jim was an experienced world traveler. His 187 extended business and pleasure trips had taken him to every part of the world and every town in the United States with a population of more than five thousand.

Described as a dandy by local citizens, he always appeared in public immaculately attired in solid white or striped suits, spats, and jewelry. From his very noticeable gold-capped teeth to his fingers adorned with diamonds, rubies, emeralds, and other precious stones, he resembled a walking jewelry store. His favorite walking stick, studded with diamonds, was but one of the four hundred he owned. Always armed, for good reason, he carried a gold-plated, pearl-handled Smith & Wesson pistol, a gift from his friend Mr. Wesson.

Diamond Jim threw extravagant parties at his mansion. Dignitaries from afar attended these grand affairs. Inside the house, they enjoyed unbounded hospitality. At one party, the visitors were shown trunk after trunk of jewels. The host invited them to run their hands through the precious gems. When some fell to the floor, Diamond Jim smiled and said glibly, "Never mind those. They were probably not as heavy with carats as the others."

The festive days and glamorous nights came to a sudden halt when Diamond Jim died of a cerebral hemorrhage on July 15, 1952, in a hospital at nearby Statesville. His collection of priceless mementoes was sold at public auction to settle his estate.

Almost thirty years later, Diamond Jim's mansion was abandoned and hastening to ruin. Had it not been for the generosity and foresight of Hiddenite native Eileen Lackey Sharpe, the old wooden palace would have probably become a memory. In 1981, she purchased the house and established the Hiddenite Center.

One of the purposes of the center is to interpret the

mansion's storied history. In addition to paid staff, there are ghosts who assist in the interpretation.

For example, a spirit lives in the room where Diamond Jim stored his precious stones. Some believe its mission is to protect the one-time treasure house.

Even more strange are the sounds associated with the third-floor room where the Civil War bugle belonging to Diamond Jim's father was stored. People have heard beautiful music coming from the room. Could that music be phantom notes from the bugle of which the senior Lucas was so very proud? Could it be the melancholy tune that J. F. Lucas played for Lee and Grant when the Southern cause was lost?

And there is the steady *tramp, tramp, tramp* that often breaks the silence of the same room. No other explanation being readily available, the sounds are said to be the marching footsteps of Diamond Jim's father and his Confederate comrades as they made their way to that fateful encampment at a place called Appomattox.

A room on the second floor is haunted by a ghost that pre-dates Diamond Jim's ownership of the house. Those who have encountered the apparition of a beautiful woman here have sensed an evil aura about her. One eyewitness heard the ghost exclaim, "Beware! Beware!" She seems to be intent on maintaining possession of the house. Might this haunt be the heartbroken Margaret, who was never able to live in her honeymoon cottage, at least in her lifetime?

The meticulously restored Victorian structure now known as the Hiddenite Center exists as a foundation affiliated with Appalachian State University. The mission of the foundation is to perpetuate local history and culture. The first-floor museum and the second-floor art gallery are open to the public. Visitors can tour the grand old home for a nominal fee. Though it appears that the master of the house rests quietly in the grave, the place speaks eloquently of his days as a bon vivant. And if you choose to take the tour, don't be surprised if you meet up with one of the spirits who have refused to leave the elegant confines of Diamond Jim's mansion.

THE STRANGER

The greater part of our evils are not real but imaginary.

Saint Francis De Sales

WHATEVER THE SEASON, the mountains of North Carolina are known far and wide as some of the most beautiful in all of America. Once the automobile emerged as a popular mode of travel in the twentieth century, roads and parkways were constructed to make the mountains more accessible to tourists. Nonetheless, there remain isolated ridges, coves, and valleys in the remote reaches of western North Carolina where few outsiders have trod. It is in these insular places that witches and other supernatural entities are said to live.

One of the tourists drawn to the North Carolina mountains in the late nineteenth century was Woodrow Wilson, who had spent a portion of his youth in the eastern part of the state. In 1885, the future American president brought his bride here for their honeymoon. During their stay, Mr. and Mrs. Wilson developed a deep interest in the fascinating and often frightening stories of witches in the mountainous part of North Carolina. Some of these tales involved eccentric old ladies who, simply because of their unsightly physical appearance and unconventional behavior, were branded as witches. Others involved women possessed of such wicked character and evil powers that there could be little doubt as to what they were. Somewhere in between were the stories of strange, mysterious women who might have been witches. This tale from Alleghany County, handed down by local storytellers, has as its main character such an individual. So you be the judge.

Stretching from the southwestern corner of the county to its center, the Peach Bottom Mountains are a series of majestic grass-covered slopes that rise to four thousand feet. As they are now, these mountains were a place of spectacular natural beauty in 1870. But times were hard that year. Even though Alleghany County had not been a battlefield during the Civil War, it was plundered by lawless deserters, bushwhackers, and Yankee raiders. Once the war ended, Reconstruction did little to improve the economic outlook of farmers attempting to eke out a living.

One such farmer was a young woman known in the community as Miss Betsy. Her farm was located by one of the myriad creeks at the base of the Peach Bottom Mountains. Miss Betsy's plight was one that an unmarried lady such as she should not have had to bear: her father was blind; her mother was an invalid; all of the family's former slaves had left the farm; and only one hired hand, an untested worker, was available to take care of the countless daily chores. Miss Betsy was willing to labor in the fields and barns to make the farm viable, but her infirm parents required her constant attention. As the summer wore on, the fields went untended and the place fell into disrepair. Things had reached a crisis when *she* came.

She seemed to appear out of nowhere just as Miss Betsy was hanging out the laundry one morning. Miss Betsy first noticed the elderly woman as she negotiated the foot log over the creek that separated the farmstead from the meadow. As she drew nearer, it became apparent that she was not from these parts.

She and Miss Betsy came face to face near the grape arbor. What a peculiar-looking individual she was! Tiny in stature, the woman could not have weighed a hundred pounds; she was ancient; her hair, although still black as coal, was ever so thin; her skin, greatly wrinkled, gave her the look of a shriveled prune; and her piercing black eyes added to her mysterious aura.

When she asked Miss Betsy for a drink of water, the young lady handed her a gourd filled from the well. Sensing that the old woman was fatigued, Miss Betsy invited her to sit and rest a spell.

Despite the woman's unappealing physical appearance, she seemed to be harmless. When Miss Betsy asked her if she had traveled a great distance, the woman responded in vague terms: "Maybe yes, maybe no." Before Miss Betsy could become annoyed at the evasive answer, she was startled and mystified by the next words from the woman's mouth: "You are in need of help, and I have come to offer that help."

At that moment, there were many things Miss Betsy wanted to know. How could a complete stranger know about the need for help at the farm? Who was this queer, ugly little woman?

Her query only brought another cryptic answer: "No person told me. I have other means of learning things. And I come from no place in particular."

Finally, the woman got to the point and provided a name and a proposal: "I will answer to the name of Miss Duncan. I want no money. I will work for my board and keep. I will do you no harm. And I will serve you well."

As she surveyed the old woman's delicate condition, Miss Betsy tempered her excitement at the prospect of getting badly needed help. But how could she refuse the kindly offer?

Then came ominous words from Miss Duncan: "When I leave, I will go as I came, without warning."

In spite of her reservations, Miss Betsy relented. Miss Duncan moved in and promptly went to work in the house. She performed her assigned tasks efficiently and conscientiously. Particularly pleasing to Miss Betsy was the mysterious visitor's uncanny ability to anticipate any household problem before it occurred. She said little and never questioned Miss Betsy's authority. All in all, Miss Betsy was delighted with the assistance. As a result, she paid little attention to her farm hand, who argued that Miss Duncan was a witch. He went so far as to claim that she caused him great distress at night by causing cats to roam about his bed.

Miss Duncan was a loner. She wanted nothing to do with neighbors and visitors. When someone called at the farm, she made herself scarce.

Accordingly, she was bitterly opposed to assisting a local widow with her housework when the subject arose. But she had no choice, since Miss Betsy ordered her to do it. After but a few days at her temporary assignment, Miss Duncan began to skulk about the widow's house. Then unexplained, frightening things started happening in the kitchen. Deep in the night, the dishes in the cabinet began to rattle, as if an earthquake had jolted the mountains.

Anxious to determine the cause of the late-night commotion, the neighbor woman lay in wait with a candle one evening. As soon as the dishes began to clatter, she hurried toward the cabinet. Abruptly, the noise ended. But when she went to bed and extinguished the light, the racket commenced anew.

On another night, the widow tiptoed to the cupboard while the dishes rattled. When she reached the cabinet this time, the noise did not abate. The brave woman groped for the cabinet door and jerked it open. A cat-like creature leaped from the cupboard and rubbed against her legs. But it was no ordinary cat. Rather, it had a slick, slippery feel. The widow attempted to stomp the creature before it vanished into the blackness of the night.

The following morning, Miss Duncan reported that she was ill, and the widow was only too happy to send her back to Miss Betsy. Almost instantly, the eerie story of the cupboard spread throughout the area. That gossip, coupled with the tales told by Miss Betsy's hired hand, caused hysteria in the Peach Bottom Mountains. The truth appeared to be self-evident: Miss Duncan was a witch! As a consequence, every bad thing that happened to anyone in the community was attributed to the little old woman.

Faced with increasing complaints from her neighbors, Miss Betsy came to the realization that she had to dismiss Miss Duncan. On the morning she was to send the woman packing, Miss Betsy walked into the kitchen and found the breakfast table set and the coffee perking as usual. But Miss Duncan was not on the job. Anxious to find her, Miss Betsy knocked on her bedroom door repeatedly. When there was no response, she opened the door and slowly entered the room. On the bed, she found the lifeless, tiny body of the strange woman. In vain, Betsy called out her name.

Miss Duncan had kept her promise: she had gone as she had come, without warning.

Witch or not?

STAIRWAY TO HELL

Speak of the devil and he appears.

Italian proverb

GEOGRAPHIC FEATURES and places that bear the name of the devil are found in all parts of North Carolina. There are more than twenty-five of these spots—creeks, unusual rock formations, and even sites where the devil is said to have paid a visit. Some of the most famous—or infamous—are the fabled Devil's Tramping Ground in Chatham County, the Devils Court House in the Great Smoky Mountains, and the Devils Garden along the Wilkes County-Alexander County line, a rugged, rocky area where rattlers and copperheads thrive. But of all the places named for Satan, the most haunted may very well be the Devil's Stairs in Ashe County.

From West Jefferson, the county seat, NC 194 snakes its way north toward the Virginia line on a route that parallels the tall mountains synonymous with Ashe County. Approximately six and a half miles north of West Jefferson, a highway bridge spans Buffalo Creek near the junction with SR 1507 (Stanley Road). Towering above the span on the left is an unusual granite formation that looks like four nearly perfect rock-stair steps. Each gigantic step is almost twelve feet high. This place, long known to locals as the Devil's Stairs, is one of the most ominous supernatural sites in America.

Scientists believe that the mountains of North Carolina are some of the oldest, if not the very oldest, in North America. However, in geologic terms, these unusual rock steps are of relatively recent origin. They came into being in 1914 as a result of dynamite blasting during the construction of the Norfolk-Western Railroad line that ultimately ran from Abingdon, Virginia, to Todd, North Carolina. Although the railroad was abandoned in the 1970s and the tracks subsequently taken up, the old rail bed is clearly visible on the east side of the highway at the Devil's Stairs.

When work on the railroad got under way at this site, dynamite was loaded into an enormous rock that stood in the right of way. A black laborer lit the fuse and attempted to run to safety, but he fell in the process. The ensuing explosion killed the unfortunate man. According to old-timers in the area, parts of his body were found in the adjacent forest for days. Some area folks, believing that Satan had a hand in the terrible accident, quickly gave the stairs their forbidding name. And it was not long after the man's death that the first of many frightening stories associated with the place began to circulate. People who lived nearby claimed that they could hear the ghost of the dead man singing old-time gospel songs as he walked along the railroad. Those reports were followed by eyewitness accounts of a headless man roaming the Devil's Stairs.

A second death that took place within a year of the

construction accident added to the haunted aura. A steel bridge preceded the concrete span that stands at the site today. The tragedy occurred when a young mother stood on a giant rock beneath that steel bridge and tossed her unwanted infant into the swirling waters of Buffalo Creek. Not many days after the youngster drowned, fishermen along the creek began to hear the phantom cries of a child in distress.

Then came numerous chilling reports of spectres at the Devil's Stairs. On a black night not long after the railroad was constructed, Jim Pullman, a resident of Warrensville, a small community just north of the rock stairs, was returning home on his horse following a visit with a neighbor who lived south of the old bridge over Buffalo Creek. As he neared the haunted spot, visibility was virtually nil. Suddenly, something was there in the middle of the road at the base of the Devil's Stairs! Pullman's horse came to an abrupt halt to avoid running into a casket bearing a corpse. Try as he might, Pullman could not coax his spooked mount to move around the coffin. Anxious to reach the security of his home, he dismounted and attempted to lead the animal past the roadblock. But the horse would have none of it. Finally, Pullman realized he would have to spend the night at the home of a friend who lived nearby. His host later described Pullman when he knocked at the door that night: "You coulda wrung water out of his clothes, he was that scared and runnin' so hard." When the morning sun brought light to the Devil's Stairs, the yet-unnerved man mustered enough courage to resume his trip home. When he came to the spot where his journey had come to an abrupt halt the previous evening, there was no casket to be found. No one was ever able to explain the bizarre occurrence. Local people claimed that the casket was that of the dead railroad laborer, whose ghost roamed the nearby tracks.

Soon thereafter, a second horseman, W. T. Wilcox, had an even more frightening encounter at the Devil's Stairs. Wilcox, a highly respected physician, was journeying home on a dark, bleak night when he suddenly felt something jump on his horse from behind. Before he could look over his shoulder to ascertain the identity of the unwanted passenger, two hairy arms made their way around his waist. His terrified horse broke into a full gallop. When it reached Oak Grove Baptist Church, located about a half-mile south of the Devil's Stairs, the unknown creature vanished.

A similar incident was experienced by W. T. Dollar, a horse-back-riding tobacco salesman for the R. J. Reynolds Tobacco Company. After completing his appointed rounds late one afternoon, Dollar started out on his usual route home, which took him past the Devil's Stairs. By the time he reached the site, nightfall had overtaken him. Suddenly, something leaped out of the darkness onto his horse behind him. The terror-stricken animal bolted down the road. Oddly enough, when it reached Oak Grove Baptist Church, the horse stopped without its master's urging. As in the case of Dr. Wilcox, the mysterious presence on the rear of the horse had disappeared without a trace. Dollar goaded his horse into walking the remaining three-quarters of a mile home. As soon as he dismounted, he tried to calm the jittery animal, only to discover upon close inspection that there were strange marks on its flanks. They resembled chalk outlines in the shape of somebody's legs. Whatever it was that had hitched a ride at the Devil's Stairs that night had left behind the impression of its legs pressed against the body of the horse.

Over time, the horse gave way to the automobile as the primary mode of transportation on the road that winds past the Devil's Stairs. Still, the haunting incidents continued. One night in the 1930s, a local group that included W. T. Dollar, Thad Porter, Ed Porter, and Slim Elliott decided to park the Model-T Ford in which they were riding in a small clearing near the Buffalo Creek bridge and the Devil's Stairs. Refreshed by the cool evening air, the friends were enjoying conversation when the apparition of a pretty lady attired in white appeared from the creek below. As the startled men watched, the ghost vanished. They quickly drove away.

Since that time, the ghost of the mysterious lady in white has been observed many times. There is speculation that she is the mother who drowned her child in the creek. One night some years ago, Lyn Goss of Warrensville found himself near the huge boulder where the child had been thrown into Buffalo Creek. The only sounds breaking the stillness were the wind and the rushing water. And then he heard it—the unmistakable cry of a baby emanating from the creek. As disconcerting as the cries were, a greater fright was forthcoming when Goss came face to face with a spectral woman in white who floated out of the woods and began pursuing him. He ran as hard as he could until the ghost vanished near Oak Grove Baptist Church.

For many years, motorists traveling NC 194 at the Devil's Stairs have picked up hitchhikers who turned out to be phantoms. Other motorists have looked into their rearview mirrors to see uninvited backseat passengers who subsequently vanished into thin air. These supernatural encounters began in the 1930s after a tragic death occurred on the curve at the Buffalo Creek bridge. A stranger hurrying toward West Jefferson was unable to negotiate the curve, and his vehicle carried him to a violent death when it crashed into the rocky creek. In the wake of the accident, people driving past the Devil's Stairs late at night began to report a common terrifying experience. Time and time again, drivers peering into their rearview mirrors would see a strange man sitting in the backseat. But upon turning around to get a good look, the motorists would find no one there.

One credible Ashe County resident experienced the terror of the Devil's Stairs in recent times. The lady was employed as a dispatcher for the Jefferson Police Department. En route to her late-night shift, she heard the rear door of her car open and then close as she drove across the Buffalo Creek bridge. Gripped with fear, she thought that someone had entered her vehicle. But when she looked into the backseat, it was empty. A law-enforcement officer described her appearance when she arrived at the station: "She was as white as a sheet."

Folks in these parts claim that the face of the devil can been seen in the waters of Buffalo Creek. This eerie phenomenon was first observed after the strange death of John Crebs in the mid-twentieth century. Crebs, a local farmer, enjoyed roaming the area's mountainous terrain. On one of his walks, he is said to have come face to face with the devil!

One foggy morning, Crebs set out on the treacherous climb up the steep granite slope in search of a missing calf. In the course of his ascent, a scraping sound in a rhododendron thicket attracted his attention. Pulling back limbs, he fully expected to find his lost animal. Instead, the overpowering acrid smell of sulfur greeted his nose, and the devil himself stepped forward. Frozen by fright, Crebs could do nothing more than look into the eyes of the Prince of Darkness. As soon as his legs would work, he fled down the mountain.

Once Crebs reached the safety of home, his wife was shocked to see that his dark hair had turned completely white. For the duration of the night, the distressed man rocked back and forth in his favorite chair and stared into space, as if in a trance. When his greatly concerned wife arose the next morning to check on her husband, he was dead.

After the sun goes down at the Devil's Stairs, the creaking of John Crebs's rocking chair can sometimes be heard. And not only does the face of the devil appear in the creek, but the smell of sulfur permeates the air when fog shrouds the mountain. Some people maintain that the devil still walks the trails on the slopes.

Phantom riders, headless ghosts, evil unknown entities, the

spirit of a drowned child, a floating apparition, and the Prince of Darkness are all said to dwell at this aptly named place. A journey to the site in daylight offers a spectacular view of the towering mountain, the strange rock stairs, and the pristine creek. But beware of a nocturnal visit here, for as longtime Warrensville resident Lula Hamby warns, "I wouldn't go past the Devil's Stairs late at night for a hundred and two dollars! I ain't that brave."

THE LONG TREK HOME

It is an honest ghost, that let me tell you.

William Shakespeare

IN SEPTEMBER 1780, Captain Robert Sevier, a giant of a man, departed his home at the Nolichucky settlement in what is now eastern Tennessee with a group of frontier Patriots called the Overmountain Men on a mission to strike a blow for American independence on the Carolina frontier. He left behind a young wife and two small sons.

As it turned out, Captain Sevier and his compatriots were successful in their quest, but the fortunes of war were such that he was not able to return to his home and family. Today, after more than two hundred years, the soldier, who stood seven feet tall, may yet be trying to make it back to his home across the mountains. He, or at least his ghost, has been encountered numerous times on an isolated stretch of highway in Avery County.

Attired in their traditional hunting shirts, the Overmountain Men were led by Robert's intrepid brother, John Sevier, and several other distinguished colonels. They joined forces with Patriots from the foothills of the Carolinas and Virginia to overwhelm the fearless Scottish officer Patrick Ferguson and his large force of Loyalists at the Battle of Kings Mountain on the North Carolina-South Carolina border on October 7, 1780.

Most historians agree that the battle marked the turning point of the Revolutionary War. Sir Henry Clinton, the longest-serving British commander in chief during the war, described the defeat at Kings Mountain as "a fatal catastrophe." But it was Thomas Jefferson, the third president of the republic born of the war and the chief architect of the document that declared America's independence, who said it best when he wrote about the battle, "It was the joyful annunciation of that turn of the tide of success which terminated the Revolutionary War with the seal of our independence."

As the fighting at Kings Mountain was drawing to a bloody close, Robert Sevier sustained a gunshot wound in his kidney as he was reaching for a ramrod. After Dr. Johnson, a captured British surgeon, failed in his attempt to extract the shot, he dressed the wound and advised Captain Sevier that the ball could be removed later, if the patient would remain immobile and quiet for a while. On the other hand, if Sevier were to promptly strike out for home, the physician predicted that the damaged kidney would become infected and lead to his death in nine days.

Sevier, a fierce and independent frontiersman, feared capture by the enemy more than death itself. Even the remonstrations of his brother and commander, John Sevier, to remain behind were of no effect. Hardly able to mount his horse, the badly wounded soldier set out for home in the company of his nephew, James Sevier.

On the ninth day of their long, arduous journey, the two

men reached Samuel Bright's place, located near the banks of the Toe River in what is now Mitchell County. They camped near the same spot where the Overmountain Men had bivouacked on their march to Kings Mountain. After the Seviers ate a meager meal, the weakened Robert fell desperately ill. Just as the surgeon had predicted, he died. James Sevier wrapped the body of his uncle in a blanket and interred it in the shade of what he described as "a lofty mountain oak." He placed fieldstones to mark the grave.

On September 9, 1951, the Daughters of the American Revolution held an elaborate ceremony to dedicate a tombstone at the grave site. Although the oak was long gone by that time, Sevier's grave, located on private property, was readily identifiable because of its unusual size. The headstone and footstone were separated by a distance of nine feet.

Local folks familiar with the area where Captain Sevier died and was buried swear that his spirit left the grave long ago and walks along US 19E in southwestern Avery County near Plumtree, a community three and a half miles from where he succumbed to his wound in 1780. On numerous occasions over the years, unwitting pedestrians walking that remote route have sensed the eerie presence of someone following them. Upon turning around to look, the walkers have found no one there.

Old-timers in this part of Avery County are quick to say that "the following haunt" is the ghost of Robert Sevier. It is believed that his spirit cannot rest because his body lies many miles from his home and family, far across the Blue Ridge. To this day, the spirit follows unsuspecting persons walking northwest along US 19E. It is said that Captain Sevier is trying to make it back to the Nolichucky settlement.

Further credence is lent to the story by reputable local citizens who have heard the distinct sound of an approaching horse that never appears. Forty years ago, a local man named Clark

Stafford was riding his horse when he heard the unmistakable *clip-clop* of the invisible animal. So terrified was Stafford's mount by the supernatural sounds that it threw him.

Apparently, the riderless horse is the phantom of the mount that belonged to Captain Sevier. According to accounts of the death, his nephew encountered stubborn resistance from Robert's horse, which balked as it was being led away to begin the trip home without its master. Could it be that the ghost of the animal patiently trots up and down the road waiting for Robert?

Motorists who stop to stretch their legs or get a breath of fresh mountain air along that lonely portion of US 19E near the Toe River might be advised to listen very closely for the sound of an ancient war-horse. They might also sense the spirit of a fallen American military hero. After all, Captain Robert Sevier may still be on that long trek home.

THAT WHICH NO MAN COULD TEAR ASUNDER

What beckoning ghost along the moonlight shade
Invites my steps, and points to yonder glade?

Alexander Pope

MOUNT PISGAH, the majestic 5,721-foot peak located in Buncombe County near its boundary with Haywood County, provides a breathtaking view of distant points in North Carolina, South Carolina, Tennessee, Georgia, and Virginia. Annually, thousands of visitors make their way to the mountain via the Blue Ridge Parkway to avail themselves of the natural beauty that is little changed since the first white settlers came to this part of the North Carolina mountains. Many years ago, a tragic story unfolded here that claimed the lives of two young lovers. Their ghosts continue to haunt the slopes of Mount Pisgah. Indeed, the very likeness of the newlyweds enhances the winter beauty of the mountain.

When General Griffith Rutherford arrived here in the summer of 1776 to lead his expeditionary force against the Cherokees, he brought with him the Reverend James Hall, a talented soldier and Presbyterian minister from Iredell County. Standing atop the mountain that reached more than a mile into the heavens, Hall was astounded by the panoramic view of the French Broad River Valley. It called to mind the mountaintop view of the Promised Land that Moses enjoyed after the forty-year ordeal in the wilderness. Moses had stood on the summit of Mount Pisgah, and it was that same name that Hall decided to bestow upon the mountain where he stood.

Almost one hundred years later, another visitor to western North Carolina climbed to the top of Mount Pisgah and was likewise awestruck by what he beheld. As a result, he decided to use his enormous wealth to purchase thousands of acres of the surrounding countryside. Below the mountain peak, the millionaire constructed an expansive hunting lodge. Some miles east, near Asheville, George Vanderbilt erected his castle, Biltmore House, the largest private home in the world.

Between the visits of James Hall and George Vanderbilt to Mount Pisgah, countless settlers established homesteads on the slopes and in the valleys and glens of what is now Pisgah National Forest. Two of the families who put down roots here were the Strattons and the Robinsons. The bittersweet tragedy that was played out when their paths crossed not only provided Mount Pisgah with two ghosts but also enhanced its natural beauty in winter.

Jim Stratton, a handsome young man, lived with his mother near Big Bald Mountain, located south of Mount Pisgah. Across the ridge on the other side of Frying Pan Gap lived pretty Mary Robinson on her father's homestead. Growing up, Jim and Mary saw each other only a few times a year when they attended services at a little meeting house in one of the coves between their homes. On those occasions, neither paid much attention to the other. But by the time Jim was seventeen and Mary fifteen, there was a change in their relationship. Jim noticed that Mary was no longer a little girl. Almost by magic, it seemed to him, she had been transformed into a shapely young lady with lovely, dark brown hair and stunning brown eyes.

Although he was shy around women, Jim made it a point to pay regular visits to the Robinson farm just to be near the radiant Mary. Soon, small talk between the two gave way to words of affection. All the while, Mary's father kept an eye on the infatuated couple. He did not like Jim. Some folks believed it was because Jim operated a still in an ivy thicket near Bull Ridge. But almost every farmer in this part of the mountains—including Mr. Robinson—ran a still in order to get a return on their corn crops. Whatever the reason, just as he had done with Mary's previous suitors, Old Man Robinson forbade Jim to come back on his property.

Unlike those other boyfriends, Jim refused to stay away. Instead, he decided to stake out the Robinson still so he would know when Mary's father was there. The young man would then hurry to the ridge behind the Robinson cabin, where his bobwhite-like whistle would summon his beloved Mary. His plan was perfect. Day after day, the couple enjoyed romantic walks about the beautiful mountain forests.

Mary was smitten with Jim, but she pleaded with him to stay away for fear of incurring the wrath of her father, who had a quick temper. Her pleas fell on deaf ears, for Jim Stratton was a tough mountain lad with a stubborn streak himself. He meant to have Mary for his wife.

Jim had a disgust for legal authority that had grown since the local sheriff killed his father when Jim was a little boy. Quite naturally, then, his blood boiled one day when he heard that revenue agents were coming to destroy his still.

Convinced that Mr. Robinson had turned him in, he hurried to the ridge and called Mary, using their special whistle. Quickly, the young woman ran to him, only to be greeted by threatening words: "Iffen them revenuers ax up my still, I'm a-fixing to settle with your pappy."

Mary believed with all her heart that her father had nothing to do with the raid. But she knew that violence would ensue if she and Jim stayed around. She suggested that they run away together. As appealing as the idea was, Jim would have none of it at the moment, so determined was he to have a showdown with Mr. Robinson.

It was a cold afternoon just about dark in mid-December when the revenue agents and their dogs descended upon Jim's still. Using their axes, the lawmen began to smash the barrels of white lightning that Jim had produced. Meanwhile, the owner of the operation watched from behind an enormous oak tree, his rifle poised. When the revenuers started demolishing the still itself, Jim took aim, squeezed the trigger, and sent a bullet into the forehead of one of the men. With that, he fled the scene, intent on seeking a confrontation with Old Man Robinson.

En route, he stopped at the house of Peggy Higgins, a neighbor lady, to tell her what had transpired. A close friend of Jim's mother, Peggy wanted to do all she could to help the boy. She urged Jim to forget about settling the score with Mr. Robinson. She suggested that to avoid capture, he must leave the county immediately. But the hardheaded Jim would not listen. Instead, as he prepared to leave for the Robinson farm, he requested that Peggy hurry and bring Preacher Ball up from the cove. Jim promised that he would return with Mary in two hours. Peggy knew Jim well, so she did as he asked.

As the young man hiked toward the Robinson place, a heavy snow began to fall. By the time he reached the special ridge, two inches covered the ground.

Mary was waiting for him. No sooner had he given a whistle than she was in his arms. Her beautiful face was filled with worry. "Jim, you must go away, and you must hurry and not lose no time," she said. "The law's done been here, and Pappy went with 'em, and they're going for more men, and they're meaning to take you, Jim, dead or alive."

Jim consoled his girlfriend with a warm embrace and words of hope and promise: "Mary, honey, in a way I'm sorry your pappy's not here, and in a way I'm glad. You go and get your things, and we'll go to Peggy Higgins's house, and Preacher Ball will be there, and we'll be wedded, you and me, and we'll go somewheres and set up, and we'll never come back here no more."

Mary sprinted to the house. Within a few minutes, she came back out, her mother and brother trailing and calling her name, to no avail.

Walking as close together as they could to keep warm in the ever-worsening weather, the young couple made the trip to Peggy Higgins's cabin. No one was home, which led Mary to worry that Peggy had not located the parson. They waited and waited some more. Finally, after an hour, Peggy and Preacher Ball arrived.

Jim expected the minister to chide him for his wrongdoing, so he was surprised when Preacher Ball made only a simple inquiry as to whether he had a ring. That question sent Peggy Higgins into a tizzy. She scurried about the cabin as if on a scavenger hunt. From under her bed, she pulled out an old white dress and a yellowing veil. Her face beaming, Peggy handed them to Mary and said, "This here's what I was wedded in, and I'm aiming that you shall have it and be wedded in it, same as I was." She then removed from her finger a gold ring, handed it to Jim, and said, "That'll be your wedding ring, too."

There was no time for Jim and Mary to admire their gifts, for they heard the sound of barking dogs at that very moment. Someone was coming. Mary implored Preacher Ball to perform the ceremony, and he responded by promptly pronouncing the couple to be husband and wife.

As the newlyweds kissed to seal their vows, the shouting voices of men disturbed the sweet occasion. Jim broke from the embrace to look out the cabin door. He saw his pursuers fast approaching. In an instant, Mr. and Mrs. Jim Stratton were gone.

When the men and dogs arrived at the Higgins place, neither Peggy nor the preacher let on that they knew anything. By the time the posse left, darkness had swallowed up the mountainside. And to complicate matters for the search party, the snowstorm had become a blizzard. There was no sign of the fugitive couple.

Waist-deep snow covered the mountain slopes when the cloudy morning broke. Still, there was no sign of Jim and Mary.

It was not until the spring thaw that searchers on Mount Pisgah discovered what was believed to be the bones of the young lovers. Officials reckoned that they had frozen to death in the blinding storm on their wedding night.

But most folks in these mountains don't put much stock in that official report. For on frigid winter nights when a full moon casts its glow, the ghost of a young man can be observed cuddling the ghost of a young woman. And when snow has fallen on the north side of the mountain, it mysteriously forms a most special pattern—that of a man and woman. If you should ever happen to see it, you will have seen Mary and Jim Stratton, the bride and groom of Pisgah.

THE RESTLESS PROSPECTOR

It is good to love the unknown.

Charles Lamb

MOST MOTORISTS driving along US 64 in southwestern Burke County pass through Brindletown without knowing it. Were it not for the sign on the volunteer fire department, this historic community would go completely unidentified. Without question, the small, quiet village in the North Carolina foothills is a mere shadow of what it was in the first half of the nineteenth century.

Gold was Brindletown's claim to fame. The discovery of that precious metal in the community came courtesy of a down-and-out stranger who showed up in Burke County one day in 1828. Sam Martin, a New Englander of Irish descent, had been fascinated from a young age with the search for gold. Accordingly, he had traveled to South and Central America to prospect—and, in the process, to deplete his resources. Devoid of money and hope, Sam set out on foot for home.

Residents of Brindletown did not know what to make of the

vagabond who suddenly appeared in their village. Sam's clothing was by then reduced to rags, and he had long ago replaced the soles of his boots with the bark of trees.

In Brindletown, he called at the home of a cobbler, who graciously took him in. During Sam's stay, the family of the shoemaker was captivated by the stories of his travels and adventures. His storytelling prowess drew attention throughout the village. Most every night, the cobbler's home was filled with neighbors eager to hear Sam spin tales of faraway places.

In time, the visitor to Brindletown regained his strength. Not wanting to wear out his welcome, Sam accepted the new shoes and clothes offered by his hosts and announced that he would take leave of the village on the morrow.

However, when he arose the next morning, he noticed golden flecks glimmering in the mud chinking of the cobbler's cabin. Sam knew immediately that he had found the magical metal that had eluded him for so long. He called for the shoemaker, who told him that the mud came from nearby Silver Creek, a tributary of the Catawba River. Confidently, Sam related to his friend that there was gold to be found in the area.

Working together in the creek, the two men brought up gold almost each time they placed their pans on the sandy floor of the stream. In hopes of keeping their discovery a secret, they conducted their work at night under the light of pine torches.

But the strange commotion at the creek soon attracted hordes of curious villagers. The secret was no more. Prospectors descended on Brindletown like locusts, and the village became a boom town overnight. Shortly thereafter, gold strikes were made in the adjoining counties of McDowell and Rutherford. Over the next decade, gold mining was the dominant industry in this part of the foothills. From 1830 to 1840, the Bechtler Mint, a private mint sanctioned by the federal government, operated in nearby Rutherfordton to take advantage of the gold that the visitor to Brindletown had found.

Sam Martin remained in Brindletown for six months after his amazing discovery. Convinced that he had amassed a fortune sizable enough to last him a lifetime, he decided once again to leave the community that had given him a new lease on life.

He departed Brindletown in grand style. Nattily costumed in a black top hat, a tailored suit, and fine footwear—quite a contrast to his attire when he had entered the village—Sam said farewell to his many grateful friends and climbed aboard a new coach loaded with leather bags filled with North Carolina gold. Then, with the crack of a whip, Sam Martin left Brindletown for good, en route to his first stop at Morganton.

Sam never made it to the seat of Burke County or to his home in Connecticut. He and his coach were never seen again. What happened to Sam on the road to Morganton remains an unsolved mystery. The most plausible explanation is that he was a victim of robbers who lay in wait to kill him and steal his gold.

Since Sam's disappearance, people who live along the road from Brindletown to Morganton have reported hearing the faint sound of hoofbeats and the creaking of a coach that never appears. The longstanding tradition in this part of Burke County is that the eerie noise is that of the ghost of Sam Martin, who is still trying to get back home with the riches he found in the Old North State.

THREE GRAVES IN HAPPY VALLEY

But she is in her grave, and, oh,
The difference to me!

William Wordsworth

IN 1958, the Kingston Trio released its version of an old American folk ballad, "Tom Dooley," which skyrocketed to the top of the popular music charts in the United States and achieved great commercial success around the world. Based upon a sordid love quadrangle that ended in the hills of western North Carolina during the early days of Reconstruction, the traditional ballad concludes with the haunting lines: "Killed poor Laura Foster / Don't you know you're bound to die." Even more haunting is the lingering mystery related to the flesh-and-blood Tom Dula (pronounced Dooley) and his three paramours, one of whom met her tragic, bloody demise on a ridge near the Yadkin River at the Wilkes County-Caldwell County line. The execution of Dula for the murder and the subsequent eerie death of another of his lovers were both tinged with elements of the supernatural. And the ghost of the murder victim is said to appear at Dula's grave on occasion.

Ironically, the setting for this tragic melodrama of lust, depravity, jealousy, and homicide was a place long known as Happy Valley. Stretching sixteen miles from Patterson, a small town in central Caldwell County, to Ferguson, a community in western Wilkes County, the fertile river valley attracted prominent early settlers. In the course of his exploration of the North Carolina mountains during the summer of 1828, Professor Elisha Mitchell, the famed scientist from the University of North Carolina, recorded a description of Happy Valley: "This upper valley to the Yadkin is delightful; from a half mile wide, bounded by ranges of mountains of moderate size, the Brushy Mountains on one side and a small chain parallel to the Blue Ridge on the other; the land is very fertile, pleasant to cultivate . . . ; the air is salubrious and healthy and the soil occupied by very respectable farms."

The *New York Herald*'s coverage of Tom Dula's execution, which occurred forty years after Professor Mitchell penned his notes about the area, included a contemporary description of the residents of Happy Valley: "The community in the vicinity of this tragedy is divided into two entirely separate and distinct classes. The one occupying the fertile lands adjacent to the Yadkin River and its tributaries, is educated and intelligent, and the other, living on the spurs and ridges of the mountains, is ignorant, poor, and depraved. A state of immorality unexampled in the history of any country exists among these people, and when such a system of freelovism prevails it is 'a wise child that knows its father.' " While the *Herald* reporter may have been a bit harsh and stereotypical in his assessment of the local people, he gave a hint of the licentious lifestyle of the primary players in the enduring mystery, Tom Dula and three young women who were cousins— Laura Foster, Ann Foster Melton, and Pauline Foster.

In eastern Caldwell County, travelers can observe a small,

white, fence-enclosed grave in a pasture alongside NC 268, the highway that snakes its way through Happy Valley. Buried here in a spot close to the tenant farm where she grew up is Laura Foster. Ever since Friday, May 25, 1866, when the twenty-two-year-old woman died of a knife wound to the chest on the nearby ridge that now bears her name, the haunting question of who killed her has begged for a conclusive answer.

Tom Dula, who, according to the traditional ballad, "Took her on the hillside / Stabbed [her] with a knife," made his way home to Happy Valley as a gallant Southern soldier at the conclusion of the Civil War. His service record in the Confederate army was an admirable one. In March 1862, three months before his eighteenth birthday, Dula had volunteered for duty and was assigned to the Forty-second North Carolina, the regiment to which he was attached for the duration of the war. His unit rendered conspicuous service in the bloody battles at Bermuda Hundred, Cold Harbor, and Petersburg. In January 1864, Dula, an accomplished fiddle player, was listed on the muster roll as a musician. A little more than a year later, while fighting as a member of General Robert F. Hoke's division near Kinston, North Carolina, he was captured by Union forces and imprisoned at Point Lookout, Maryland. Upon his release from prison on June 11, 1865, Thomas C. Dula began the long journey to his mother's cabin on Reedy Branch near the small Wilkes County community of Elkville.

As the *Herald* put it in 1868, Dula, "though not handsome might be called good-looking." He stood almost six feet and had dark, curly hair and dark eyes. Although he returned to Happy Valley a war-hardened twenty-one-year-old veteran, one thing had not changed about Tom while he fought for the South in faraway places: his insatiable desire for pretty women. Some of his fellow soldiers hinted that he may have murdered the husband of a Wilmington woman with whom he had an affair during the war. And upon his return home, Mary Winkler, one of his valley neighbors, gave the opinion that he was a "no-account scoundrel, but a charmin' dandy."

Prior to going away to fight as a teenager, Tom had been quite the ladies' man. From his mid-teens until his departure for war, he had maintained an intimate relationship with Ann Foster, who lived with her mother in a cabin just north of the Dulas. Lotty Foster, Ann's mother, publicly stated that she had discovered Tom and her illegitimate daughter in bed together in 1859, when both were no more than fifteen years old. "I recognized him," she recalled. "He jumped out and got under the bed. I ordered him out. He had his clothes off."

By all accounts, Ann Foster was a young lady of striking beauty. Her petite figure, soft, milky-white skin, and black hair turned many a head in Happy Valley. Even the reporter for the *Herald* seemed to be captivated by her when he wrote, "She is entirely uneducated, and though living in the midst of depravity and ignorance, has the manner and bearing of an accomplished lady, and all the natural poise that would grace a born beauty."

Ann Foster could have had any man she wanted, but Tom Dula, it seems, was her first and only love. Nonetheless, when he went off to war, she did not wait for him. Instead, she married James Melton, a well-respected cobbler and farmer in Happy Valley. Apparently, she was never in love with Melton, who was a number of years her senior. Their marriage was one of convenience.

Despite her marital status, Ann resumed her passionate love affair with Tom not long after he returned to the North Carolina mountains in 1865. And they were not discreet about it. Tom would frequently spend the night at the Melton place, which was located on Reedy Branch north of the Dula homeplace. Inside the Melton cabin were three beds. James slept in one, Ann slept in another, and Pauline Foster slept in the third. Pauline, a cousin of both Ann Foster Melton and Laura Foster, was about their same age. Around the first week of March 1866, she made her way from her home in Watauga County over the mountains to Happy Valley to seek treatment for syphilis from a local physician, Dr. George N. Carter. While there, she accepted employment in the Melton household in order to pay for her medical care.

When Tom Dula came calling, it was under the pretense of his interest in Pauline. At bedtime, Tom and James would retire to the same bed. But as soon as James was fast asleep, Tom would crawl into bed with Ann. Meanwhile, Pauline developed a crush on Tom.

While Tom was only too happy to share intimate moments with Pauline, he did not return her affection. Rather, his special feelings were reserved for Ann and another cousin, Laura Foster. His emotional rejection of Pauline caused bitter jealousy that may have prompted her to provide damaging testimony in Tom's trials for murder.

Whether Tom had a sexual relationship with Laura Foster before the Civil War remains a subject of debate. But it is apparent that shortly after his postwar return to Happy Valley, the two became intimate. Laura, described by the *Herald* as "beautiful but frail," had chestnut hair, blue-green eyes, and a pleasing disposition. Pauline, who was jealous of Laura as well as Ann, downplayed the murdered woman's beauty at Tom's trials by testifying that she had large teeth with a sizable gap at the front of her mouth. Although Laura, by all accounts, had a sweet personality, she was also said to have "round heels," meaning that she was promiscuous.

By the middle of March 1866, the relationship between Tom and Laura was intense. He frequently spent the night at the cabin where she lived with her father—without any objection from him. At the same time, Tom continued his adulterous trysts with

Ann and stole time with Pauline in the Melton cabin, in barns, and in other places.

In early April, trouble began to brew when Tom was diagnosed by Dr. Carter with syphilis in its primary stage. Despite Tom's statement to the physician that he had contracted the disease from Laura Foster, historians have concluded that Pauline, the most promiscuous of the three cousins, most likely infected Tom, who, in turn, infected both Laura and Ann. Distressed by the diagnosis, Tom cooled his relationship with Laura over the next six weeks and vowed to a neighbor that he would kill the person who had given him "the pock," as syphilis was known locally. That statement would later come back to haunt him at his trials.

Not long after Tom stopped calling on Laura, the young woman visited Dr. Carter to seek treatment for her frequent bouts of morning nausea. A medical examination revealed that she was pregnant. Taking the revelation in stride, Laura, who was deeply in love with Tom, hoped that his impending fatherhood would cause him to settle down.

After receiving word that Laura needed to speak to him, Tom arrived at her cabin on the afternoon of Sunday, May 20, 1866. Laura revealed her pregnancy and expressed her love for him. Taken aback by the news, Tom told her that he needed some time to ponder the situation.

When Tom returned to visit Laura the following Wednesday, her father noticed that the couple sat close together by the fireplace in deep conversation. This time, Laura was in a state of euphoria when Tom departed. They had a plan: at sunrise on Friday, the two would rendezvous at the nearby Bates place, a deserted homestead where they had met on a regular basis. From there, they would go away to be married.

News of the planned nuptials quickly spread through Happy Valley. At the Melton place, Ann was highly agitated. She vented her rage and frustration on Pauline. Ann complained that Tom had contracted syphilis from Laura and given it to her. She swore to Pauline that she would "have do" with her husband, James, so as to make him think he had infected her with the disease. Then Ann issued a threat and a warning: she was going to kill Laura Foster, and if Pauline dared to tell anyone about their conversation, she would be killed also.

At an undetermined time early on Friday, May 25, Laura Foster was murdered on a gently sloping ridge less than a mile west of the Melton cabin. Later that morning, Ann returned home from an unspecified location and climbed into bed with Pauline. Her shoes were wet and her dress muddy.

According to Pauline, Tom showed up at the Melton residence a day later under the guise of retrieving his fiddle and getting his shoes repaired. During the visit, Ann and Tom conferred privately for almost thirty minutes. After the tête-à-tête was finished, Pauline remarked to Tom that it was her understanding that he had run off with Laura. Tom reportedly responded, "I have no use for Laura Foster."

Later that same morning, Ann informed Pauline that, in Pauline's words, "she'd done what she said." In other words, she had murdered Laura Foster.

After Laura's father reported his daughter missing, an initial search yielded no tangible results. It was not until September 1 that a party discovered a crudely dug grave five hundred yards from the Dula residence. In it was the lifeless body of Laura Foster. The corpse was resting on its side. Laura's apron had been neatly folded and placed over her face, but her legs had been broken in order to cram her body into the opening in the ground.

An autopsy performed by Dr. Carter revealed that her death had resulted from a stab wound between the third and fourth ribs near the left breast. His examination further indicated that Laura had been three months pregnant.

No one had waited, however, for the discovery of Laura's body to begin criminal proceedings. Within a week of her disappearance, Tom Dula and a half-dozen of her other suitors had fled Happy Valley in fear of being implicated. Warrants for the arrest of Tom, Ann, and Pauline were issued to the sheriff of Wilkes County on June 28.

Two weeks later, Tom Dula, working in Tennessee under the assumed name of Tom Hall, was taken into custody by his employer, Major J. W. Grayson, a former Confederate officer, near the community of Pandora. He was promptly returned to North Carolina and incarcerated in the Wilkes County Jail, where he was held for the next six weeks without bond—and without proof that Laura Foster was dead. In the cell adjacent to Tom was a person very familiar to him: Ann Melton. Pauline had been released and given immunity in exchange for her testimony against Tom and Ann.

Exactly one month after the discovery of Laura's body, a Wilkes County grand jury returned a true bill of indictment against Thomas C. Dula for murder in the first degree. Ann Melton was indicted as an accessory before and after the fact.

Zebulon B. Vance, the gifted orator and attorney who had served as a Confederate officer and as governor of North Carolina during the Civil War, acted as the lead counsel for Tom. Two important pretrial motions by the defense were granted: Tom would be tried separately, and that trial would be moved to Iredell County.

On Monday, October 15, 1866, a jury was impaneled to hear the case against Tom Dula. Twenty of the eighty-three witnesses subpoenaed by the prosecution testified at the trial. Ann Melton was present in the courtroom but was not called to the witness stand. All of the evidence presented against the defendant was circumstantial, the most damaging coming from the mouth of a woman scorned: Pauline Foster.

Just after midnight on Sunday morning, October 21, the jury commenced its deliberations. By daybreak, the twelve men—all Confederate veterans—returned to the courtroom with a unanimous verdict: guilty. At eight o'clock that morning, Judge Ralph B. Buxton sentenced the defendant to die by hanging on November 9, 1866.

Vance and his defense team gave notice of appeal to the North Carolina Supreme Court, which resulted in the postponement of the scheduled execution. On appeal, the conviction was overturned, and a new trial was ordered.

Tom's second trial began on Monday, January 20, 1868, at a special term of the Iredell County Superior Court. In essence, the evidence presented by the prosecution—all circumstantial—was the same as in the initial trial. And once again, the great orator Zeb Vance made an impassioned plea to the jurors: "The life of a Confederate soldier who has gone through the four-year war is worth a thousand wenches like Laura Foster."

For a second time, the jury did not see it Tom's way. And following that, the appeal of the guilty verdict to the North Carolina Supreme Court was unsuccessful.

At 12:42 P.M. on May 1, 1868, the condemned man was escorted from his cell in the Iredell County Jail to the waiting death cart, which bore his coffin. As the crude vehicle made its way through the streets of downtown Statesville, the throng of curious people who had assembled to witness the hanging were shocked at the demeanor of the prisoner. Tom, sporting a smile, rode atop his coffin and played his fiddle. Some observers even credited him with singing some of the words later incorporated into the folk ballad that has immortalized him.

Iredell County sheriff William F. Wasson had erected a gallows of native pine near the old Statesville train depot. At 1:08 P.M., the death cart pulled up to the hanging platform. After the noose was placed around Tom's neck, Sheriff Wasson offered the condemned man an opportunity to make a final statement. In a loud, clear voice, Tom addressed the crowd for close to an hour. To young and old alike, he offered words of advice: "You young people, watch your step and see that you don't get in the same fix. To the older folks, I'll say for you to remember that it was wine, women, and fiddlin' that got me in this here scrape." He contended that he was about to die because false testimony had been presented against him. Publicly maintaining his innocence to the very end, Tom looked directly into the eyes of the spectators, held out his right hand, and said, "Do you see this hand? Does it tremble? I never hurt a hair on that girl's head!"

For Tom Dula, time had run out. But just as he had courageously stared into the face of death on many battlefields, he bravely greeted his executioner with a smile and a bit of morbid humor: "Sheriff, this here's a mighty nice new rope you got. Reckon maybe I'd better go wash my neck so's I won't get it dirty."

At 2:42 P.M., the sheriff ordered the cart moved away from the gallows. Instantly and abruptly, Tom fell about two feet and dangled from the rope. But his neck was not broken by the fall. For more than ten minutes, his heart continued to beat as he slowly choked to death. Throughout the horrible ordeal, the dying man did not struggle. After thirteen minutes, the physician on duty at the scene declared Tom Dula dead. But the body remained suspended for an additional twenty minutes. Finally, the garish spectacle was brought to an end when Tom was cut down, put into the coffin, and turned over to his sister.

Back at the Dula homestead, the lifeless corpse was laid out on the feather bed where Tom had slept. During the night, his neck wound bled. Tom's blood remained in that room thereafter. All attempts to clean it up were in vain. A number of families lived in the cabin after it left the ownership of the Dulas. One of these families had several boys who slept in Tom's old room. They feared falling out of their bed and into "Tom Dula's blood." From the time Tom's body was brought back to the cabin until the structure was torn down many years later, it was considered haunted.

Tom was buried in a field not far from the family cabin. His grave, now marked with a modern tombstone erected after the Kingston Trio made the ballad famous, is located on private property alongside SR 1134 (Tom Dula Road), a little over a mile from its junction with NC 268 at Ferguson. Vandals and souvenir hunters have so badly chipped the marker that the site is no longer open to the public.

And what about Ann Foster Melton? To the very end, Tom refused to implicate her in Laura's death, and he apparently did all he could to keep her from being punished in the matter. On the night before he was executed, Tom allegedly penned a note in his cell, the contents of which were to be disclosed only after he was put to death. Obviously written to absolve Ann of any wrongdoing, the purported confession read, "Statement of Thomas C. Dula—I declare that I am the only person that had any hand in the murder of Laura Foster."

From the time she was arrested, Ann seemed confident that she would never be convicted. In her jail cell, she boldly proclaimed, "They'll never put a rope around this pretty neck." And she was right. Following a number of procedural delays, Ann was tried in the aftermath of Tom's execution. Zeb Vance also served as her attorney. The jurors returned with a verdict of not guilty. Maybe it was Ann's beauty that won them over. One observer certainly thought so when he opined, "Ann Melton was the purtiest woman I ever looked in the face of. She'd of been hung, too, but her neck was just too purty to stretch hemp. She was guilty. I knowed it. . . . If they'd of been any women on the jury, she'd of got first degree. Men couldn't look at the woman and keep their heads."

But perhaps there was a more sinister reason Ann Melton went free. Described as cold and calculating and possessed of a very violent temper, Ann was looked upon by the residents of Happy Valley as a wicked woman. Indeed, she was often likened to a witch. Some people were afraid of her for that very reason.

Whether she was a witch is uncertain, but there is no question that she bewitched Tom Dula with her beauty, charm, and guile. And the circumstances surrounding her death were much like those associated with the demise of a witch.

Following her acquittal, Ann lived a quiet life with her husband for five years until she was seriously injured when a cart in which she was riding overturned and crushed her. She lingered in great pain for several days. At one point, she whispered to one of the neighbor ladies who was attending her, "If I knew I would never get well again, there is something I would tell you about Tom's hanging."

As death—believed to have been hastened by her advanced syphilis—drew near, Ann summoned Dr. Carter to her room to confirm that the end was at hand. She then requested that her husband be sent in alone. With James at her side, Ann made what was presumed to be a confession in the Laura Foster murder. Rumor was that she said to him what she had said in the past to a few ladies in the neighborhood—that she had killed Laura and allowed Tom to die for the crime. But exactly what it was she confided in James will never be known, for both husband and wife took it to their graves.

Those on hand to witness the last horrifying seconds of Ann's life observed a supernatural spectacle that none would ever forget. In anguish, the dying woman screamed that she could see the flames of hell at the foot of her bed. Some say that the devil himself came that night to carry her away. Squalling black cats spitting blue fire scampered from under her bed and climbed the walls, where they offered hideous moans. Filling the room as Ann drew her last breath were strange sounds similar to hot rocks falling into cold water, along with unusual smells like that of frying meat. Shortly thereafter, her body was interred in an unmarked grave in a family cemetery close to her mother's cabin and within sight of Laura's Ridge.

With the three primary members of the strange love quadrangle in their graves, some folks assumed that this tragic chapter of Happy Valley history was over. But the controversy was only beginning. Today, lingering questions about the identity of Laura Foster's killer make the Tom Dula story one of the most chilling unsolved mysteries in all of American history. Most attorneys familiar with the case concur that Tom Dula, if tried in a modern courtroom on the same evidence presented at either of his trials, would be set free. Area residents have long maintained that Tom did not murder Laura Foster. At most, they feel he yielded to the beguiling powers of Ann Melton and helped her bury the body. Another theory, first postulated by Tom's defense team, was that Laura was killed by one of her jealous suitors. Most likely, we will never have an answer to the confounding question. Instead, it will remain buried in the three graves along the Yadkin.

Should you happen to hear the Kingston Trio's classic rendition of "Tom Dooley," be mindful that there is more to this haunting story than the unforgettable lyrics and melody. For, you see, Laura's ghost has been observed on occasion at Tom's grave. No doubt, her restless spirit longs to find out why things went so terribly wrong on that day in May so long ago, when Laura Foster was set to begin a new life with Thomas C. Dula in a place known as Happy Valley.

CATAWBA COUNTY

THE OLD COLLEGE SPIRIT(S)

And said as plain a whisper in the ear,
The place is Haunted.

Thomas Hood

MANY COLLEGE and university campuses in North Carolina
claim their own special haunt. Yet Lenoir-Rhyne College, a four-
year liberal-arts school in Catawba County, boasts not just one
spook, but rather a haunted campus.

Founded in 1891 by the Lutheran Church, the college is located on approximately one hundred acres in the heart of Hickory.
Apparitions have been seen and unusual sounds have been heard
in many of the buildings on the campus.

Some of the bizarre occurrences remain without explanation. For example, if you visit the Mauney Music Building, constructed in 1960, it is likely that you will hear footsteps in the
hallways even if no one is there. In some of the music classrooms,

the notes of trumpets and violins will greet your ears even if no human performers are present and no recorded music is being played. Because the building is relatively modern, people are at a complete loss as to the source of the eerie happenings. One female student who listened to the spectral music in the Mauney Music Building noted, "It's creepy, but you know it's not your imagination."

Folks who have encountered the ghosts in nearby Highland Hall, the oldest building at Lenoir-Rhyne, would apply the coed's assessment to this structure, too. One evening in 1985, a college employee was locking her office on the third floor of Highland when she saw the mysterious figure of a shirtless man standing in the hallway. According to the lady, the apparition had a blank look on his face. A subsequent search of the entire building by campus security revealed that all the exit doors were locked. They found no signs of forced entry and declared that Highland Hall was empty of all human occupants.

Members of a campus theatrical group using the third floor of Highland for costume and makeup rooms have reported phantom footsteps and mysterious slamming doors. Motorists driving by the old building late at night have observed a spooky light emanating from one of the rooms on the third floor.

Completed in 1907, Highland Hall now houses faculty offices, but it once served as a dormitory. The building's multiple uses over the years have provided no clues to the bizarre things that frequently take place here.

Without question, the most frightening occurrence at Highland was experienced by an alumnus who worked for campus security before becoming director of residence life. One night on his security rounds, the man made his way to the third floor, which at that time was being used for storage. No sooner had he switched on the hallway lights than they went out, leaving him in complete darkness. Stumbling back to the light panel, he tried the main switch, but it failed to work. He turned on his flashlight and had begun making his way down the hall when he heard the light panel slam shut. That was but the prelude to a terrifying display of the supernatural. Suddenly, the sounds of moving furniture filled the third-floor hall. When the guard pointed his flashlight in the direction of the noise, the beam revealed bed frames, desks, lamps, and other dormitory furnishings moving out of the rooms and into the hall. Fearing for his life, he dashed to the stairway door he had used only moments earlier to gain entry to the third floor. To his dismay, the door was locked. He promptly unlocked it and made his way out of the building without further incident.

Early the next morning, workmen from the maintenance department visited the third floor of Highland. What they observed caused them to immediately summon campus security. The hallway was littered with wrecked furniture, broken lamps, and ripped mattresses. A thorough criminal investigation followed, but it yielded no evidence of human vandals.

Among the haunted campus buildings that appear to have an explanation for their ghosts is the Carl A. Rudisill Library. Unusual things at the library have spooked students for years. Books mysteriously fall from shelves, and strange footsteps are heard in the empty stacks. But the haunt most often witnessed is the apparition of a small, sobbing child. Tradition has it that these unusual sights and sounds are the spirit of a youngster who died in a library fire years ago. Campus historians are quick to point out that there has never been a fire in the existing library building, which was completed in 1943. However, the library was previously housed in the Old Main Building, a structure that was destroyed by a blaze in 1927. Books and other materials salvaged from that inferno are now housed in the Rudisill Library. Consequently, some people believe that the spirit of the child has made its way into the current facility.

Over the years, students studying in the library have reported hearing the faint sound of a crying child. Particularly late at night, patrons have also observed the apparition of a small boy dressed in tattered clothing of an earlier time. On one recent occasion, a number of campus visitors noticed what appeared to be a small lad, attired in little more than rags, standing outside the library near the air-conditioning equipment. When they approached the child, he fled and vanished into thin air.

There may be an explanation for the ghost in Schaeffer Hall, too. Numerous students have had terrifying encounters with the apparition of an elderly lady who makes periodic bed checks on the second floor of the dormitory. In 1978, a coed came face to face with the transparent figure of a matronly woman who was in the process of checking doors. When the ghostly lady looked up, she scowled at the student, put her hands on her hips as if disgusted, and disappeared before the young woman's very eyes.

Based upon the descriptions provided by eyewitnesses of the ghost of Schaeffer Hall, longtime Lenoir-Rhyne employees believe the apparition is that of Mrs. Ona Piery, who served as house mother at the residence hall. For years, she lived on the second floor of Schaeffer, where she could most often be seen rocking in her favorite chair. In 1973, Mrs. Piery was forced to move to another housing complex when Schaeffer was converted into a male residence hall, over her vehement objections. Two years later, Mrs. Piery died of natural causes. Since that time, her ghost has frequently been seen walking the halls of Schaeffer or enjoying her favorite rocking chair there.

Should you find yourself in Hickory, take the time to visit historic Lenoir-Rhyne College. But beware that wherever you go on the beautiful campus—whether it be the Music Department, the faculty offices, the library, or Schaeffer Hall—you are likely to encounter the old college spirits.

THE GIANT BLOODSUCKER

A monster, which the Blatant beast men call,
A dreadful fiend of gods and men ydrad . . .

Edmund Spenser

FEW ANIMALS in all of nature are considered more revolting than the leech. Generally found in bodies of water, these ugly, flattened annelid worms are equipped with a sucker at each end. Although science down through the years—including modern medicine—has found the leech to be useful in the treatment of various human maladies, the very thought of the creatures is enough to evince a look of discomfort in most people. Because of its distasteful appearance and its proclivity to attach itself to the human body in order to suck its blood, the leech has been a popular subject for horror and science-fiction films. For example, *The Leech Woman*, starring Grant Williams, terrorized American moviegoers when it was released in 1960.

But what if, outside of the safety of the theater and its silver-screen monsters, a giant leach really existed? If Cherokee tradition is to be believed, an enormous red-and-white-striped leech lived on the Valley River in Murphy, the seat of Cherokee County. In fact, the Cherokee name for Murphy is *Tlanusiyi*, which means "Leech Place." Whether the monster leech—described by the Cherokees as being as large as one of their houses—still exists is not known. But there is a place on the Valley River just above its junction with the Hiwassee River that is known to this very day as the Leech Place.

According to the Indians, there is a deep hole in the river at this site. Nearby, a ledge of rock used by past generations of Cherokees as a bridge runs across the river. On the south shore, a trail once climbed a high bank that afforded a magnificent view of the water. It was from this vantage point that a group of Cherokee men spotted the gargantuan leech lying on the rock ledge. Uncertain what the massive object was, the men watched in bewilderment and horror as it unrolled. When the creature stretched itself out on the rock, its red and white stripes were clearly visible. Momentarily, the leech rolled up in a ball again. Then it stretched once more. Finally, it crawled down to the river and vanished into the depths. Suddenly, the water foamed and boiled, causing a tall waterspout to form. Had the terrified Indians not fled the scene, the great column of water would have carried them into the river, where certain death awaited.

Other Indians were not quite so fortunate as the first eyewitnesses. Soon after the mammoth leech was observed, Cherokees began finding the lifeless bodies of its victims on the riverbanks. When the corpses were examined, it was discovered that their noses and ears had been devoured.

Fear spread throughout the area. Everyone chose to avoid that portion of the Valley River—except for one foolhardy individual. Scoffing at the tales of the giant leech, the fellow proclaimed that he feared nothing and announced that he would visit the Leech Place. After applying paint to his face and dressing in his finest buckskin outfit, he set out for the river as his friends and neighbors watched cautiously from a safe distance. En route to the rock ledge, the Indian could be heard singing: "*Tlanusi gané ga digi gage / Dakwá nit lasté sti*" ("I'll tie red leech skins / On my legs for garters"). But when he was about half-way across the natural bridge, his merry song ended abruptly as the water began to boil. In the blink of an eye, he was swept into the river by a massive wave and was never seen again.

In 1838, many of the Cherokees in western North Carolina were forcibly removed to the Oklahoma Territory. Several years before that cruel, chaotic, and painful event, two daring Indian women ventured onto the ledge at the Leech Place to go fishing. Disdaining the admonitions of the villagers, one of the women, who carried her baby on her back, proclaimed, "There are fish there, and I'm going to have some. I'm tired of this fat meat." When it came time to bait her line, the woman placed the child beside her on the rock. Before her very eyes, the water boiled and started to wash the helpless infant into the river. Had it not been for the mother's lightning-fast response in pulling the child to safety, it would have been another victim of the giant leech.

Although the creature was seen only that one time above the water, the Indians maintained that it lived in the deep hole in the river. When they peered down into the water at the Leech Place, they could see a large living creature on the bottom.

Does this monstrosity or one of its offspring still live in the depths of the Valley River? No one really knows. There have been no reported sightings of the beast in more than 150 years. But on the other hand, no diver has been bold enough to search the floor of the river. Perhaps the mountain waters of North Carolina at the Leech Place, much like the mountain waters of Scotland at Loch Ness, will forever hide a mysterious creature that is completely unknown to science.

THE VOICES FROM BELOW

When you have solved all the mysteries of life you long for death, for it is but another mystery of life.

Kahlil Gibran

FOR TIME IMMEMORIAL, humans have considered a voice heard from above to be a good sign, a manifestation of divine intervention. On the other hand, a voice heard from below carries a sinister connotation, for either it is coming from the dead in the grave or from Satan deep in the pits of hell. But the voices that come from below the pristine mountain waters of western North Carolina are believed by the Cherokee Indians to belong to a race of benevolent spirit people called the Nunnehi, otherwise known as the Immortals.

Picturesque Shooting Creek rises in southeastern Clay County and flows west until it opens into expansive Chatuge Lake on the Hiwassee River. The name of the creek comes from the Cherokee word *du-stagalan'yi*, which means "where it makes great noise." Today, the waterway is a relatively tranquil place.

But if you listen closely near its mouth, you just might hear people talking below.

To the Cherokees, the Nunnehi were not ghosts or gods. Rather, they were spirits of supernatural human beings that generally remained invisible. As late as the nineteenth century, however, some of the Immortals appeared to the Indians of western North Carolina as fairies and little people. These happy spirits enjoyed music and dancing. Cherokee braves were often drawn to the sounds of their revelry. But upon their approach, the commotion would suddenly shift to their rear or to another direction. Never could the braves find the site of the dancing. The Immortals were seen only when they wanted to be seen.

Years before the Cherokees were driven from their homes in Clay County and other parts of the North Carolina mountains, the Indians along the Hiwassee and Valley Rivers heard the voices of the Nunnehi proclaiming words of warning. For days on end, the unseen Immortals foretold the conflicts, turmoil, and misery that the Cherokees were to face. After finally gaining the Indians' attention, the friendly spirits offered words of assistance: "If you would live with us, gather everyone in your townhouses and fast there for seven days, and no one must raise a shout or a war whoop in all that time. Do this, and we shall come, and you will see us, and we shall take you to live with us."

At a hastily convened council, the Cherokees who lived near the mouth of Shooting Creek discussed the proposal. All agreed that the Immortals were a happy and good people. The decision was an easy one. Unwavering in their trust of the Nunnehi and fearful of the misfortune that was surely to come, the Indians prayed and fasted as directed. On the seventh day, a loud roar from the distant mountains made its way closer and closer until the waters of Shooting Creek grew rough. There was great fear among the Indians until the Immortals suddenly appeared and took the people to live with them under the water.

Since it was created in 1942 by a dam on the Hiwassee at the mouth of Shooting Creek, the ten-mile-long Chatuge Lake has been popular with swimmers and boaters. Cherokee fishermen still use the picturesque body of water. When they drag for the bounteous quantities of fish near Shooting Creek, where lake depths reach 140 feet, their nets often get caught on the bottom. But this inconvenience does not upset them, for the fishermen know it is caused by their ancestors pulling on the nets as a reminder that they should not be forgotten.

Should you have occasion to visit the scenic eight-thousand-acre lake on a bright summer day, be sure to make your way to the mouth of Shooting Creek. If you peer into the deep waters and listen very carefully, you just might hear the voices of the ancient Cherokees, as well as those of the Immortals who took them to the safety below the surface almost two centuries ago.

CONTENTED GHOST

Everything has its wonders, even darkness and silence.

Helen Keller

MOST GHOSTS have a raison d'être. They purposefully haunt or linger at places that were important in the lives of the human beings they now represent in spirit form. In the annals of supernatural North Carolina, ghosts have manifested themselves for a variety of reasons: to guard or protect their haunts or the people or property located at the site; to exact revenge; to right a wrong or to otherwise obtain justice; to communicate love or other human emotions to the living; to warn people of danger; to search for missing objects or body parts; or simply to tarry at a place cherished by an unfortunate person whose life was ended prematurely through tragedy.

But what happens when a ghost achieves its purpose? In most cases, it no longer makes its presence known at the site it haunts. Whether the ghost actually ceases to be is beyond human knowledge. This tale from Cleveland County involves just such a ghost.

In the summer of 1973, the future was bright for Mr. and Mrs. Ray Bridges, both graduates of Western Carolina University, as they looked for a home in Cleveland County after completing their service in the Marine Corps. One day not long after they started their search, Ray's father invited his son and daughter-in-law to ride over to look at an old farmhouse that was being used for yarn storage. The place was located near Polkville in the western part of the county. As it turned out, the one-story, seven-room frame structure was a special place for Ray's dad. It had belonged to his grandfather.

When Ray and his wife purchased the abandoned, dilapidated late-nineteenth-century farmhouse built by Reuben Bridges, Ray's great-grandfather, they had no idea that the ghost of old Reuben haunted the place. From all outward appearances, the weather-worn house was gloomy and hastening to ruin. No one had lived there in twenty years. Windows were broken; paint had long peeled away; and the place lacked all modern conveniences. But Mrs. Bridges was taken with the house; to her, it had possibilities. A closer inspection revealed that Reuben Bridges had built the sturdy home of heart pine. Mrs. Bridges reasoned that, with hard work and vision, the run-down structure could be transformed into a charming showplace.

Ray was a bit reluctant to undertake such a massive remodeling project. However, his wife's excitement about the house caused him to accede to her wishes. Over a period of weeks, they used their spare time to make the house livable once again. One of their first chores was to remove the porch, which had been added at the back of the original structure. It was in bad condition and was not of the same quality as the house. Not long after they accomplished this task, eerie things began to happen.

As the list of incidents grew during the succeeding weeks, neither Ray nor his wife could explain what was going on. Perhaps it was vandals or prowlers. First, there were phantom slamming doors. While the couple was painting in a front room one evening, they heard the distinct sound of doors closing at the rear of the house. Unsure of who had come in, Ray investigated. No one was around, but all of the doors at the back were standing wide open. On another occasion, Mrs. Bridges was busy cleaning a floor when a strange noise attracted her attention. She jumped back just as a heavy door fell off its hinges and toward her.

As the long-anticipated moving day neared, an employee of a pest-control company came to spray the house while Mr. and Mrs. Bridges were away. The couple had made arrangements for the exterminator to obtain the house keys from Ray's mother. Upon doing so, he made his way to the renovated structure, where, much to his surprise, every door in the place was unlocked. After finishing his work, he made no effort to lock the doors, assuming Mr. and Mrs. Bridges intended for the house to be left open. But when the couple arrived later that day, every door was locked tight.

Before retiring for their first night in their remodeled home, Mr. and Mrs. Bridges checked all the doors to ensure that they were secure, given the unusual occurrences of recent days. Around two o'clock in the morning, they were startled from their slumber by the unmistakable sound of footsteps inside the house. Ray climbed out of bed and looked all about, but he found no intruder or anything out of order. When they awoke in the morning, every door in the house was standing open.

In the days that followed, the same spooky thing happened again and again.

About two weeks later, Ray and his wife had occasion to chat with an elderly neighbor who had been acquainted with Reuben Bridges as a child. The neighbor graciously presented them a framed photograph of Ray's great-grandfather. In the course of the conversation, Mr. and Mrs. Bridges were informed that Reuben and his second wife had argued about whether the back porch should be built. Reuben had been against the idea, but after he died, his widow had gone ahead with the project anyway.

Upon returning home with the photograph of Reuben, Ray and his wife decided it would be a nice touch to display the likeness of the family member who had built their beloved home. They proudly hung the picture in the entrance hall. From that moment, they were never again bothered by any mysterious incidents.

No other explanation being readily available, it would seem that the ghost of Reuben Bridges haunted the old house until it got its way. By removing the porch that Reuben so disliked, Mr. and Mrs. Bridges had no doubt pleased the ghost. And when they gave Reuben's framed picture a place of honor in his former home, now newly restored, the ghost was obviously satisfied. In death, Reuben Bridges prevailed; his old home was just as he wanted it. Accordingly, his ghost, having accomplished its purpose, may be no more. Or perhaps it still abides here, invisible, silent, and oh so contented.

THE GHOSTLY CHANT

Let the chant be full of gravity; let it be neither worldly, nor too rude and poor. . . . Let it be sweet, yet without levity, and while it pleases the ear, let it move the heart.

Saint Bernard of Clairvaux

FEW REMAIN NOW, but well into the nineteenth century, numerous stone cairns could be found along the ancient trails in the Cherokee country of the North Carolina mountains. Designed by the Indians as a method of interment and a way to memorialize the place of burial, these sepulchral monuments were constructed of large stones piled loosely together to a height of six feet or more. According to Cherokee tradition, each passerby was to add a stone to the grave. But after white settlers took up residence in the western part of North Carolina, virtually all of the cairns were violated and destroyed by treasure seekers.

Most of the pyramid-shaped stone monuments that once lined the old trail on the ridge from Robbinsville, the seat of Graham County, to the Valley River in northeastern Cherokee County have been leveled. Some of the cairns were constructed almost a decade before the American colonies declared their independence. Interred at those sites were a number of Cherokee women and children slaughtered by an Iroquois war party before a peace treaty could be finalized between the two Indian nations in 1768. Legend has it that, even though the graves have been badly desecrated over the years, the chanting voices of women and children can yet be heard in the area. Perhaps the haunting chants are the dirges of those murdered Indians. More likely, however, they are a song of gratitude for the retribution sought and claimed by Chief Talédanigíski and his warriors.

The name Talédanigíski means "Hemp-Carrier." The Indians used hemp to make thread and cordage. Hemp-Carrier was the chief of the Cherokee settlement in the Cheoah Mountains of Graham County. When he received the grim news of the terrible carnage caused by the Iroquois attack on helpless members of his tribe, he swore revenge. After putting together a group of warriors that included the father of Junaluska—the legendary chief who was to follow—Hemp-Carrier set out after the murderers.

Days turned into weeks as the Cherokee war party made its way across the rugged terrain of the Great Smokies. In the course of their march, the Cherokees surprised an Iroquois war party that was headed south. Hemp-Carrier was not satisfied until every enemy warrior was killed and scalped.

On trekked the revenge-minded Indians from the North Carolina mountains. They hunted their adversaries until they found them far to the north. Darkness was falling one evening as Hemp-Carrier and his band, positioned in a well-hidden spot, watched the activities in the Iroquois town. Their anger mounted as they witnessed a hideous spectacle: the Iroquois women danced over the scalps of the Cherokee victims and gave loud shouts of celebration.

During the ceremony, a sizable group of the dancers walked down to the spring to refresh themselves. At that point, the Cherokees emerged from their nearby position and delivered silent but lethal blows to the unwitting victims. When the slaughter was complete, Hemp-Carrier could count as many scalps as had been taken from the Cherokees. All the while, the dancing ritual continued in the village.

Not yet sated, Hemp-Carrier gathered his braves and addressed them with fiery language: "We have covered the scalps of our women and children. Shall we go home like cowards, or shall we raise the war whoop and let the Iroquois know that we are men?"

One of the men shouted in a voice of defiance, "Let them come if they will!"

From the mass of excited Cherokees came a loud war cry and yells for more scalps. Almost immediately, the dancing in the village ceased. Hordes of enemy fighters armed with guns and hatchets sprang from the town house. But the attackers could find no one. Hemp-Carrier and his fleet-footed men knew the trails too well. They escaped and made their way back to the safety of the Cheoah Mountains without losing a single man. For his bravery and leadership in achieving the victory, Hemp-Carrier was acclaimed a hero and rewarded with seven wives. Retribution was indeed sweet for the Cherokee chieftain.

If you have occasion to drive south out of Robbinsville on NC 129 as it winds its way alongside Tulula Creek, be sure to listen for strange sounds in the pristine setting. What you hear might not be the croaking of the frogs for which the creek was named, or the wind that often whistles or howls or shrieks through these mountains, or the scream of a mountain lion or the lonely hoot of an owl. Instead, it might be the ghostly chant of triumph, the celebration of the spirits of the slaughtered Cherokees laid to rest here more than two hundred years ago.

THE EVIL EYE

Evil enters like a needle and spreads like an oak.

Ethiopian proverb

BEGUN IN 1936 as part of President Franklin D. Roosevelt's economic recovery program, the Blue Ridge Parkway is an elongated national park that has as its centerpiece a magnificent roadway along the crest of the Blue Ridge Mountains. From its beginning at Shenandoah National Park in Virginia, the route stretches 469 miles to Great Smoky Mountains National Park in North Carolina and Tennessee. More than half of its mileage is in North Carolina.

One of the many visitor centers located along the parkway is a small facility at Milepost 451.2 in Haywood County near its border with Jackson County. It stands in the shadow of Waterrock Knob, a majestic 5,718-foot peak. From the center, a trail leads hikers on a strenuous climb to the top of Waterrock, where, on clear days, they are treated to a spectacular 360-degree view of the Blue Ridge, Cowee, and Balsam ranges to the east and south, the Smokies to the west and southwest, and Mount Mitchell fifty miles to the northeast.

Few people who enjoy the awe-inspiring beauty of Waterrock Knob realize that the mountain overlooks the former cabin site where one of the most haunting tales in North Carolina history was played out in the distant past. Indeed, one of the principal players in that macabre drama may still haunt the mountain.

Oconee Sheen was fifteen years old when it all began. She lived in a crude cabin at the base of Waterrock with her cruel father, Peter Sheen. They both had thick, reddish hair. But in most every other respect, the two had nothing in common. In fact, Oconee hated her father.

Any love she ever felt for the man had evaporated years earlier when her beloved Cherokee mother, Alca, was laid to rest on the mountainside amid the blooming rhododendron, honeysuckle, and mountain laurel. At the grave site, Peter Sheen had offered an outburst of laughter for every tear that Oconee shed. Following Alca's burial, Peter abused Oconee both verbally and physically. On one occasion, he threw her to the floor, causing permanent damage to her back. But the worst was yet to come. In a fit of rage one dark day, Peter Sheen administered a savage beating with his leather whip. One of the wicked lashes caught Oconee's right eye, causing such irreparable damage that it had to be removed. Oconee filled the cavity of her lost eye with a large, radiant gemstone. But the teenager knew she would forever be disfigured and would never be a woman of striking beauty like her mother. Day by day, her contempt for her father intensified.

Finally, in the stillness of a dark mountain night, Oconee took an ax and hacked her father to death while he slept. She then pulled up the boards of the cabin floor, threw the bloody body of Peter Sheen under the dwelling, covered it with dirt, and replaced the flooring. Oconee walked outside and breathed the fresh mountain air. She felt no remorse. If anyone inquired about Peter Sheen, she would reply that he had returned to his people. At last, she was free!

Years passed. As Oconee grew older, she became uglier in physical appearance. Even her false eye changed, increasing in radiance. Meanwhile, she developed frightening powers. If she looked at a singing bird, it would immediately fall dead. Her strange eye caused plants to wither and die. When she made her way by neighboring cabins, children ran inside and dogs howled, all in fear of the evil that was Oconee Sheen.

No one ever saw her do any work, yet she never seemed to lack for anything. Whatever she needed, she took with her mysterious powers. Those neighbors who refused her demands paid a heavy price. Down in the valley, old Joe Martin rued the day he did not give Oconee the ham she asked for. The woman cast her bad eye at him, then pointed her index finger at his field of golden wheat, ripe for harvest. It immediately burst into flames. Another incident involved a minister from the tiny Jackson County village of Willits, who visited the Waterrock area once a month to preach to the people there. When he informed Oconee that she was possessed by the devil, she cast her evil eye and pointed a finger at him. The parson fell dead.

Oconee's neighbors looked down upon her as a half-breed. As her reign of terror grew, they made every effort to avoid her. Yet no one was safe. Word quickly spread about little Agnes Murphy, a neighborhood girl. The tiny lass made the mistake of laughing at Oconee's twisted, deformed back. Oconee fixed her evil right eye on the hapless child, pointed her index finger, and spoke some strange words. Agnes tried to call out for help, but instead, she quacked like a duck.

Time marched on. As Oconee's age mounted, so did her

hatred and bitterness. Because of her physical disfigurement, she had a great contempt for all things beautiful. She hated men because of the abuse wrought by her father. She hated children because of their happiness and laughter. In short, Oconee hated herself.

One day, she fell seriously ill. Dr. Wayne Morton, a physician from Willits, was summoned to her bedside. A fire was slowly dying in the fireplace as the physician bent to check Oconee's pulse and temperature. As he examined her, his attention was drawn to her right eye, which shone like glistening ice. Before Dr. Morton could say anything, Oconee remarked in a rather matter-of-fact way, "I am dying." When the doctor nodded in agreement, the old woman cackled and offered her final haunting words: "You say I'm dying, but you are wrong. Oconee never dies. Even death cannot keep me in the grave." With that, her good eye closed. Dr. Morton could detect no pulse or heartbeat. As he placed the covers over Oconee, the fire suddenly went out, and the cabin was engulfed in darkness.

Oconee was buried on the mountain beside her mother. Strangely enough, all of her neighbors came to see her laid to rest. But no one sang or offered a eulogy or a prayer. As the crude wooden coffin was lowered into the ground, a cloud covered the sun. A dog howled in the distance.

The day after the burial, Dr. Morton paid a visit to Joe Martin and posed a curious question: "Were you ever close to Oconee Sheen?"

Befuddled by the query, Joe shook his head and said, "I always stayed as far away from her as I could."

Excitement building in his voice, Dr. Morton said, "So did I, until the night I examined her. But that night, I discovered something. You know her eye, the right one?" Joe nodded. "It's a stone, all right," the physician continued. "Why, man, it's a diamond as big as a hickory nut! When I leaned over her, the firelight caught it, and it almost blinded me. All these years, she's gone about the hills with a fortune in that socket." With Joe now hanging on every word, Dr. Morton got to the point: "Yes, and now it's buried out on a lonely mountainside. What shall we do about it?"

Without hesitation, Joe replied, "Go get it. Now, tonight!"

The nighttime sky over old Waterrock Knob was unusually dark when Joe Martin and Dr. Morton arrived at the Sheen cabin. Upon reaching the grave site, the two began digging furiously. But when they reached the coffin and began to lift it out, Dr. Morton thought he heard a voice saying, "Oconee never dies. Even death cannot keep me in the grave."

With great trepidation, the doctor lifted the lid as Joe held the lantern. Both men were greatly relieved to see the body of Oconee just as it had been laid to rest. Nonetheless, it took every bit of his courage for the physician to reach into the casket and pull the diamond from the eye socket.

As he started to move away with the prize, something cold grabbed his wrist. Dr. Morton looked down to see Oconee's fingers clutching him in a death lock. As he stood there, immobilized by fear, the corpse unleashed an awful scream, threw her arms around him, and pulled him into the coffin. Tossing the diamond to Joe, Dr. Morton cried out, "Take it and run for your life while I throttle this fiend!"

Frightened beyond description, Joe Martin took the enormous gemstone and raced to his horse. He heard gurgles coming from Oconee's grave as he galloped away.

When he reached his cabin, Joe rushed inside, locked the door, and covered the windows. As he searched for a place to hide the diamond, one of the windows flew open. A deathly cold wind blew into the cabin. And then he saw Oconee standing in the open window, a gaping hole where her right eye had been. "My eye, give me back my stone eye!" she shrieked.

Fearful of her supernatural powers, Joe threw the diamond

to her. She caught it and promptly put it back into place. For a moment, the evil eye looked at him, and Joe believed he was a goner. But Oconee merely disappeared into the darkness.

After a sleepless night, Joe returned to the grave site to look for Dr. Morton the following morning. There was no sign of him until Joe noticed that Oconee's grave had been covered again. Picking up the shovel he had used the previous evening, he carefully removed the earth from the coffin. Slowly, he lifted the lid. Inside was the lifeless body of Dr. Morton. Oconee had buried him alive!

The Sheen cabin was claimed by the elements long ago. And the graves of mother Alca and daughter Oconee—or Dr. Wayne Morton, if you will—can no longer be found in the wilderness. But no grave could hold Oconee Sheen anyway. For all we know, she still roams these mountains, for, as she said, "Oconee never dies."

THE CARPENTER

As there is much beast and some devil in man, so is there some angel and some God in him.

Samuel Taylor Coleridge

BAT CAVE, a small community in northeastern Henderson County, is well known to the tourists who travel US 64 Alternate to visit nearby Chimney Rock and picturesque Lake Lure. A low cavern on the rattlesnake-infested mountainside adjacent to the village is the habitat of bats and other unusual animals. It provided the village with its unique name.

Visitors to Bat Cave might naturally assume that any supernatural story from this village would be related to the resident bats or the dark netherworld they represent. To the contrary, Bat Cave was the setting for the visit of a stranger who some believe was the very antithesis of the Prince of Darkness.

Details of the incident were related to Manly Wade Wellman, one of North Carolina's most distinguished writers of the twentieth century, by a beekeeper from Bat Cave in 1951. Joe John

Collins's farm was located on a winding road that led up one of the mountains overlooking Bat Cave. Collins's place was one of spectacular beauty and great productivity. Terraced fields that yielded bountiful crops decorated the slopes. The barns and pastures were filled with outstanding livestock. Indeed, Mr. and Mrs. Collins had much for which to be thankful. Nevertheless, there was also cause for despair in the household: their little son, Anse, was crippled and unable to walk as the result of a wagon accident.

About noon one day, a man unknown in these parts proceeded up the steep road to the Collins farmstead and stopped at the mailbox, where Joe John was standing. The stranger was carrying a toolbox. "Wonder if there might be a job of work for me," he said. "I'm a carpenter."

Joe John was instantly taken by the man's pleasing, courteous manner. He motioned for the carpenter to join him for a short walk. "Yes. Come here across the yard. See that neighbor-house yonder?"

Gazing into the distance, the carpenter saw the other homestead, which had once been connected to the Collins place by a long footpath. Now, a deep ditch filled with water blocked the walkway. Joe John explained matters this way: "Me and the neighbor-man was like two brothers once. Then we fell out over a piece of land, and he dug that ditch to show he don't want me coming on his place." Then, in a voice filled with animosity, the farmer told the carpenter, "Now, I'll go him one better. I want you to take these planks and poles and build me a board fence along this side the ditch, so he can't even see me over here."

After a moment of quiet deliberation, the stranger remarked with a cheerful smile, "I can do something you like."

Satisfied, Joe John left the carpenter with these parting words: "All right. Now, I'm going to the upper field to chop wood. See you later."

Without delay, the carpenter went to work. As he labored, he sang songs, the words of which no one in the area had ever heard. But the soothing tunes were most pleasant to the ear. Presently, little Anse was attracted to the music. From his resting place on the couch in the farmhouse, the boy arose on his crutches and made his way out to where the stranger was singing as he worked. Anse greeted the man with a smile, and the stranger responded in like manner. The two struck up a warm conversation that lasted through the afternoon as the carpenter labored. At length, the task was finished. The carpenter accompanied the crippled little fellow back to the house to await Joe John.

When the master of the house arrived, he looked at the carpenter and asked, "All finished?" Responding in the affirmative, the stranger invited Joe John to inspect his craftsmanship.

When they got to the ditch, the farmer was shocked at what he saw. Instead of erecting a fence as he had been directed, the carpenter had constructed a footbridge across the water. But before he could express his disappointment, Joe John was hailed by his estranged neighbor, who approached him with an extended hand and words of reconciliation: "Joe John, you don't know how dog-sorry I was I dug that ditch. But now you build this bridge, Joe John, to show you never favored us being cut off."

Joe John was only too happy to shake his neighbor's hand. He welcomed an end to the feud. But he felt credit was due the man who had brought the neighbors back together. "Why, I'm just as pleased as you are. But don't credit me with the bridge notion. This carpenter here, he thought it up."

Meanwhile, the stranger was packing his toolbox in anticipation of his departure. Before he took leave of the neighbors on that late afternoon, he smiled at all present. Then, using his free hand, he touched Anse's head for a split second and said, "Throw away those crutches!"

Anse did as he was directed. Suddenly, like a deer, he bolted to his father on legs that were as good as new. His limbs were completely and remarkably healed.

Once the astonished men regained their composure, they looked around, only to discover that the wonderful stranger was nowhere to be seen. But these eyewitnesses to the miracle performed by a peacemaking carpenter in Bat Cave knew exactly who he was and from whence he had come.

TO DESTROY A THING OF BEAUTY

Where man can find no answer, he will find fear.

Norman Cousins

TUCKED DEEP in the towering mountains of western North Carolina, Jackson County is widely recognized as a place of spectacular natural beauty. Gracing its breathtaking peaks and valleys are picturesque waterfalls, pristine rivers and lakes, and magnificent trees and flowering plants. One of the most beautiful of these plants is a rare white lily that thrives in the valley that bears its name—Cullowhee. One of the oldest of all Tar Heel legends tells of the mysterious power of the Cullowhee lily.

Near the center of Jackson County at the town of Cullowhee—the home of Western Carolina University—Cullowhee Creek merges with the sluggish Tuckasegee River. South of the town, these two waterways open up the panoramic Cullowhee Valley. In early May, the landscape here appears to be covered by a spring snow, as countless lilies burst forth with their lovely white blossoms. The plant has three to seven leaves, each about three-eighths of an inch wide. Its six-petaled blossom, completely white except for a brilliant yellow stamen, reaches a maximum height of eighteen inches.

When the first white settlers reached the Cullowhee Valley during the opening decade of the nineteenth century, the lilies were abundant. Up to that time, this land had been the domain of the Cherokee Indians. To them, the lily was sacred, a special gift from their god. According to Cherokee tradition, their supreme being once walked alone in this valley during springtime. He blessed the fields to make them fertile. Every place he trod, a lily sprang up. To honor their god, the Indians called this once-nameless valley Cullowhee, which means "white lily." Every spring thereafter, the snowy blossoms returned to remind the Indians of the power and goodness of their deity. Standing atop the surrounding peaks, they lifted their arms toward the heavens and offered prayers of thanksgiving. Cognizant that the lilies covered holy ground, no Cherokee dared to pluck or trample the flowers. To do so would be to welcome bad luck, evil, or even death.

All was well until 1809, when white settlers laid claim to land in the Cullowhee Valley. One of the first was Joseph Henderson, who took up residence on the north bank of the Tuckasegee River. As May gave way to June that year, lilies covered the valley. Day by day, the Cherokee chieftain watched from his hillside village as Henderson's small children—a boy and a girl—romped about the fields with no regard to the thousands upon thousands of white flowers growing everywhere. Greatly disturbed that the sacred grounds of his people were being violated, the chief wrapped his blanket about him and made his way to the river to call on Joseph Henderson. When he reached the Tuckasegee, he could see lily petals floating in the slow-moving water.

When Henderson came to the door of his cabin, his visitor pointed to the white fields and said rather bluntly, "Evil comes to white man if he harms the lily."

Surprised by the statement, Henderson responded, "Those white flowers? What are they?"

As swift as an arrow from his bow, the chief offered words of explanation: "The white lily, Cullowhee, footprints of Chero-kees' god. God comes in spring with stars and blesses fields so grain will grow. Where he steps, the lily blooms. No man should harm them."

Henderson found it difficult to keep from laughing in the Indian's face. In a voice mixed of derision and superiority, he boldly retorted, "This is my land now. I shall pluck and plow under what I wish."

The Indian parted with words of warning: "Watch out for the boy and the girl. The lily is white, but death waits under its bloom."

Two days later, Henderson's children were at play along the valley trail. Having been told of the strange conversation between the chief and their father, the boy looked at his sister and asked, "Who believes them old Indians? I'm not afraid."

With that, he rushed into an expansive field of blooming lilies, trampling and breaking them at will. His more cautious sister watched for a while from the trail. When it appeared that her brother was greatly enjoying his romp without any harm coming to him, she reckoned it safe to pick some of the pretty white flowers along the trail. After a few minutes, she glanced out over the field to monitor her brother's activities. He was nowhere to be seen. Her calls went unanswered. Quickly, she ran home to fetch her parents.

Joseph Henderson dropped what he was doing and darted to the lily field. There, he followed a path of broken lilies to the spot where the lifeless body of his only son lay on a bed of crushed white blossoms. Nearby, he saw the culprit—a long, fat rattle-snake. Just as the chief had admonished, death awaited one who would knowingly desecrate the Cullowhee lily.

Throughout that spring and summer, the residents of the valley felt the wrath of the Cherokee god. Fields that were usually abundant yielded no crops. Even the flowers and berries that grew in the wild withered and died. And in human terms, an unexplained rash of deaths claimed numerous settlers, both young and old.

Today, the Cullowhee Valley is once again a breadbasket and a place of unbounded natural splendor. As it has for untold centuries, the Tuckasegee River winds its slow course through the valley. Every May, innumerable Cullowhee lilies explode in white along its banks. They are oh so pretty to behold, but do you dare pick one?

MILE-HIGH WITCH

Well-founded fear, which takes one through the valley of the shadow of death without abandoning one there, is what makes the worst of the worse journeys.

George Woodcock

MACON COUNTY, located in the beautiful high country of south-western North Carolina, is home to some of the tallest and most majestic mountains in the state. Seventeen peaks in the county tower more than five thousand feet, while another twenty-seven top out at more than four thousand feet.

At the dawn of the twentieth century, there lived near the summit of one of Macon's mile-high mountains one of the state's most infamous witches, Old Nance. Locals, fearing her propensity to exact revenge on any person she disliked, only whispered her name, and then with great respect. They called her Mrs. Nance.

Despite the air of secrecy that prevailed in the community

down the mountain from Old Nance's hovel, stories about the witch filtered out of the county and made their way throughout the state. A reporter from the *Wilmington Messenger* who heard some of the tales decided to launch an investigation. What he learned was intriguing.

One woman who lived in the village below Old Nance was greatly disturbed because her daughter had decided to marry a fellow from South Carolina. When the mother refused to consent to the marriage, the young lady hinted that she might elope. Mindful of the magical, albeit evil, charms of Mrs. Nance, the desperate woman took her daughter up the mountain to the witch's home as a last resort. After a brief consultation, the mother was elated to learn that Mrs. Nance detested all marriages and would do anything within her power to prevent one or to destroy an existing one. Thus, it was with little difficulty that the witch convinced the mother to leave the terrified girl in her custody.

No sooner had the mother begun her way down the mountain than Old Nance commenced her sorcery. She peeled a turnip, handed it to the girl, and forced her to eat it. As the young lady chewed, she experienced excruciating pain in her nose. Shortly, it spread to her cheek, then to her ear.

Her evil labors over, the witch returned the girl to her home down the mountain. The villagers were shocked to see that the lass's beauty was now marred by a disfigured nose. When her intended saw the unsightly change, he promptly broke the engagement and went away in disgust.

Satisfied that she had achieved her goal, the mother again took her daughter on the treacherous trek up the mountain to seek the assistance of Mrs. Nance. As before, the witch handed a peeled turnip to the disfigured girl. On this occasion, the young lady was more than willing to eat it, having been assured that it would reverse the spell. The witchcraft worked almost instantly, and her nose was restored to normal. As mother and daughter prepared to depart from the witch's lair, the old hag issued a stern warning to the girl, who was already admiring her restored beauty: if she ever again decided to marry, the same affliction would plague her.

The Wilmington reporter found a second story to be credible, too. It concerned Carn McCordle, another resident of the community down the mountain from Mrs. Nance's cabin. McCordle owned a bull that made the tragic mistake of chasing the witch when she made a rare appearance in town one day. In the midst of the chase, Old Nance stopped suddenly and came face to face with the charging steer, staring straight into its eyes with a horrifying glare. So terrified was the bull that it fled in a crazed state. Later that night, the animal started an uncontrollable bellowing and went mad in the McCordle pasture. Thereafter, it ran into the wilderness, where it became hopelessly lodged between two large trees. All attempts by McCordle and his neighbors to extricate the animal were futile. After it died and the carcass decayed, no villager was brave enough to remove its bones.

His curiosity aroused, the intrepid reporter traveled from Wilmington to Macon County in 1901. At the village, he made arrangements with a woodsman to escort him to Old Nance's cabin. Six miles into the journey, the local man could hold back his fear no longer. He declined to go any farther. Instead, he pointed the way up the mountain and said, "You can't miss it now. It ain't more'n half a mile. There's the ledge of rock, if yer sure you want to go. Don't blame me if yer friends don't know you when you come back—if you ever do get back."

Undeterred, the reporter continued the tedious climb until he reached Old Nance's cabin, which rested precariously on a sharp rock ledge overlooking an abyss that seemed to be bottomless. One look at the hag's shanty gave him a foretaste of what he was about to experience. It was a forbidding shack—a single room without windows or chimney.

Then he saw her. Old Nance, her back twisted and her skin wrinkled with age, was busy stirring some sort of concoction in a large black pot on a fire outside her cabin. Upon hearing the reporter's approach, she spun around with cat-like quickness and looked at him with a penetrating stare. After a few seconds, she broke the silence with an unusual dialect that was most difficult to understand: "Yer kin some it?"

Unsure what she meant, the reporter pulled from his pocket a silver dollar and attempted to make a sensible reply: "No, Mother, I came to hear something that you know."

The coin vanished before his very eyes, the witch spiriting it away in the bosom of her grimy dress. Peering at the stranger with a face that could only be described as terrifying, Old Nance asked, "Yer kem fer wot?"

Unwilling to give in to her intimidation, the reporter responded with firmness: "To find out if you haven't something to tell me, something about the days that are coming."

Momentarily, the witch was silent as she looked down into the nothingness below the ledge. Pointing to the abyss, she uttered words of warning: "Yer come fum below. Yer'll go back ter below."

Still trying to learn of the strange woman's powers, the fearless reporter queried, "Isn't there some charm you could give me to make it pleasanter below?"

Her grim countenance gave way to a sinister grin. She vanished into her shanty and quickly reappeared with a bowl brimming with an unknown liquid that emitted a pungent odor. To the reporter's chagrin, she offered him a taste. Having studied spells, charms, and black magic, he was reluctant to partake of the mysterious brew. Moreover, he knew that numerous poisonous plants thrived on the mountain where Old Nance lived. Using all his guile, he looked at the witch and said in a very mannerly way, "It isn't polite to drink alone. After you."

His measured response invoked the hag's ire. She threw her brew to the ground, stormed into her cabin, and barred the door. With that, the reporter's audience with Old Nance was over. Sensing that his well-being might be in jeopardy, he took leave of the place.

Following his arduous descent of the mile-high mountain, the man walked into the settlement, where the astonished villagers greeted him "as one from the dead," in his words. He never pressed his luck to seek another interview with the witch. And the folks in the village never learned what happened to her after that. For all they knew, she vanished into thin air!

BLOODY MADISON

War would end if the dead could return.

Stanley Baldwin

DURING THE CIVIL WAR, Madison County acquired a repugnant nickname: "Bloody Madison." Because of its isolated location on the mountainous Tennessee border, Madison was not in the forefront of the major military engagements of the titanic conflict that pitted American against American and North Carolinian against North Carolinian. However, from 1861 to 1865, a true state of civil war plagued the county. Its citizens engaged in and were subjected to a reign of bloodshed, violence, pillaging, arson, and terror the likes of which have not been witnessed since. At the site of a long-vanished log cabin in the northern part of the county, there lingers today a ghostly reminder of the time when death and mayhem were the order of the day in Bloody Madison.

From Buncombe County, the scenic but powerful French Broad River slices Madison diagonally as it flows northwest into

Tennessee. One of the principal tributaries of the French Broad in northern Madison is the Laurel River, sometimes known as Laurel Creek. The valley of the Laurel was the setting for the Civil War events that led to the county's unpleasant moniker and its lingering haunts.

The great majority of the citizens of the Laurel Valley were sympathetic to the Southern cause. Men and boys from the area joined with others from Madison County to form a number of military companies that were mustered into the Confederate army. While these soldiers were away on active duty in distant theaters, the bloody civil war in the Laurel Valley involved Union and Confederate forces comprised mainly of soldiers from the mountains of North Carolina and Tennessee. But to make matters worse for the women, children, and old men of the valley, there was a third faction in the turmoil. Alternately called outliers or bushwhackers, these lawless men were army deserters and renegades who fought, killed, maimed, raped, plundered, and burned for neither side, but only for themselves.

From the early days of the conflict, Madison County was terrorized by outliers. According to the *Official Records* of the war, the Laurel Valley was a "district in Madison County long known as a general resort and hiding place for outlaws." In early 1862, a group of these ruffians, self-styled Union sympathizers, poured over the mountains from Greene County, Tennessee, and took up residence at the head of the Laurel. Led by "Captain" Dave Fry, they launched a series of wild raids on homesteads up and down the river. In response to the cries of outrage from law-abiding citizens who had been robbed, threatened, and assaulted, Confederate forces initiated a series of reprisals that temporarily halted the atrocities.

By early January 1863, however, the outliers based in the Laurel Valley were back at work. A band of fifty descended on Marshall, the county seat, where they plundered a number of mercantile establishments and ransacked the home of Colonel L. M. Allen, a prominent Confederate officer of the Sixty-fourth North Carolina.

To avenge that crime, Lieutenant Colonel J. A. Keith, a native of Marshall, was given field command of a two-hundred-man Confederate expeditionary force. During the last half of January, Keith sent his soldiers up and down the Laurel Valley to round up men and boys who were suspects in the attack on Marshall. A group of thirteen old men and boys was captured with little or no resistance. Three days after the roundup, the prisoners were escorted to a secluded spot on the Laurel River, where they were ordered to take a seat on an enormous log. A firing squad stepped forward and executed the entire group, whose members ranged in age from thirteen to fifty-six. All the bodies were unceremoniously dumped into a hastily dug trench.

News of the so-called Shelton Laurel Massacre spread through the county like wildfire. Reports of the indiscriminate slaughter of thirteen civilians without benefit of trial were greeted with indignation from all quarters. Governor Zeb Vance, a stalwart Confederate who had grown up on the banks of the French Broad in Buncombe County, was appalled to learn that eight of the thirteen had not even participated in the attack on Marshall. He appointed a special investigator, who later reported, "Such savage and barbarous cruelty is without a parallel in the State and I hope in every other."

In a letter to the Confederate secretary of war, Vance denounced the actions of the Southern troops as "a horror disgraceful to civilization." Newspapers in the North had a field day with the incident. Even a journal in Germany, the *Westliche Post*, took note of the event and proclaimed Lieutenant Colonel Keith "a monster, for he spares neither age nor infancy."

A little more than a year after the massacre, Union forces exacted harsh revenge in the Laurel Valley. In April 1864, Colonel George Washington Kirk, a Tennessee Unionist, led two regiments of local Yankees the Second and Third North Carolina Mounted Volunteers—on a hunt for families who were loyal to the Confederacy. Just east of what is now the community of Guntertown, they came upon the cabin of Nance Franklin, a widow. Three of her sons who actively sided with the Confederates happened to be at home. The badly outnumbered Franklin boys fought valiantly against the raiders but were killed. Mrs. Franklin narrowly escaped death when a bullet clipped a lock of her hair. She screamed in agony as the soldiers departed after torching her cabin. Moving on, the marauders attacked another cabin on the banks of the Laurel. This family, whose name has been lost to history, was not quite as "fortunate" as Nance Franklin. Though their cabin was not set afire, it was looted, and each family member was killed.

Some years after the war, when peace and civility had returned to the Laurel Valley, two local men happened to be passing by that second cabin late one evening when the stillness of the mountain night was disturbed by screams and moans. Assuming that someone had moved into the cabin, the men hurried to render assistance. But when they peeped in a window, they saw no signs of life. They hastened to the front door as the cries grew in intensity. It was wide open, so the would-be rescuers entered. In the front room, they encountered a dim figure that appeared to be that of a young woman. "Please help me!" she pleaded.

Spooked by what they had seen and heard, the men rushed toward the door, only to be confronted by a group of ghost-like soldiers on the front porch. Their guns were aimed at the unfortunate fellows. The two then rushed back into the front room, only to find that the apparition of the young woman had vanished. When they turned back toward the phantom soldiers, the ghost troop was also gone. A thorough search of the cabin produced no living human beings.

Other people later experienced similar supernatural sights and sounds at the cabin. Finally, the place was deemed haunted, and residents of the Laurel Valley made it a point to avoid the site, especially at night. Over the decades, the log cabin was claimed by nature. At present, only a few logs can be found, along with several stones stained with what appears to be blood.

The ghosts of the Civil War are said to still haunt the old cabin site in the Laurel Valley. Most folks from these parts continue to stay away. And if you're wise, you will, too, for the spectres here represent the time when the county was aptly called Bloody Madison.

BUT FOR A DREAM!

All that we see or seem is but a dream within a dream.

Edgar Allen Poe

DREAMS ARE OFTEN a glimpse of future reality. Throughout history, dreams have been credited for many of the great accomplishments of the human race. Conversely, they have also provided answers to some of the great mysteries of the past. And thus it was in 1879 in the southern mountains of North Carolina.

George Feller and his sickly wife, Kathy, lived on a farm in a remote portion of McDowell County. The young farmer struggled alone to make ends meet, as Kathy was virtually an invalid due to chronic asthma. When George showed up one day at a neighboring cabin in a distressed condition, his friends consoled the sobbing man as he related the grim news that Kathy had died in the night.

Upon receipt of the report of the death at the county seat at Marion, officials there, cognizant of Kathy's medical condition, issued a death certificate even though a physician had not attended her dying moments. No physical examination of the body was ordered to determine an official cause of death.

As the time for the burial neared, the corpse was dressed and prepared for interment by neighbors, as was the tradition in this remote mountainous area. When the local parson arrived at the Feller cabin, the wooden coffin was loaded aboard a wagon for the four-mile trip to the graveyard. With the preacher in the lead, the cortege made its way slowly along the rugged route.

About halfway to the burial ground, a stranger atop a horse hailed the funeral party and demanded that it come to a halt. George Feller, his family, and his neighbors were taken aback at the audacity of the middle-aged man. Raising his hand, the man, known to not one member of the procession, spoke chilling words: "You cannot bury this woman now. She's been murdered!"

The members of the funeral party reacted to his alarming and seemingly callous pronouncement with a mixture of consternation, anger, bewilderment, and shock. Some of the more outspoken neighbors challenged the stranger to prove his dark revelation. All the while, George Feller wiped his tearful eyes and pretended as if he had not heard the disturbing accusation.

Unperturbed by the hostility that Feller's friends displayed toward him, the man offered a bizarre explanation: "I don't know any of you, but I dreamed last night that on my way into this country today, I would meet a funeral procession with a coffin bearing a woman whose husband had strangled her to death. My dream told me she had been strangled with a wide leather strap. Unless you have an examination made, I'm going to report it to county officers."

Initially, the members of the burial party simply stared at the man in disbelief. But then some of them began to wonder how the stranger could have known that the casket bore the body of a woman. Perhaps it was a lucky guess. Perhaps he had heard about Kathy's death, as the news had by then spread among the peaks and valleys. Or perhaps the man, through his dream, knew something that no living person save George Feller knew.

Following a discussion, the neighbors decided to heed the warning of the unknown man. They agreed to transport Kathy's body to Marion for an examination by medical experts. George Feller interposed an objection, albeit a weak one. He argued that no one should pay attention to an unbelievable story from the lips of a complete stranger.

At the county seat, a physician took a look at Kathy's lifeless body and quickly ascertained that she had not succumbed to asthma. Instead, she had died of strangulation. His examination revealed that smooth, even pressure had been applied to her neck until she could breathe no more.

There being no other suspect, George Feller was promptly arrested and incarcerated in the county jail at Marion. The sheriff's subsequent search of the log cabin yielded the murder weapon—a broad piece of rawhide. It was found in a crude chest of drawers in the sole bedroom of the dwelling. Clinging to its edges were strands of Kathy's long, blond hair.

When confronted with the evidence, George Feller admitted that he had asphyxiated his wife. At his trial, he was sentenced to die by hanging. Later, as the noose was lowered on to his neck at the makeshift gallows outside the McDowell County Courthouse, George and many of the onlookers likely shared the same thought: "But for a dream!"

THE PREMONITION

It is bad enough to know the past; it would be intolerable to know the future.

William Somerset Maugham

HAVE YOU EVER HAD the odd feeling that you knew what was going to happen? Sometimes, that mysterious sensation does not come over you until after the event actually occurs. Suddenly, you are aware that you have seen the event before. The French call this strange feeling déjà vu, which means "already seen." But there are also infrequent times when we sense that something—usually something bad—is going to occur. Scientists refer to such exercises in foreshadowing as premonition or precognition.

Throughout history, there have been unusual individuals who seemed to possess the supernatural power of precognition. On a regular basis, these people were able to foresee events with remarkable accuracy. In the modern world, skeptics abound as to the self-proclaimed psychics who boast of their power to foretell the future. But there are few who are willing to dispute that the famed sixteenth-century French physician Nostradamus was invested with the ability to foresee and then chronicle world events that transpired centuries later.

In the aftermath of the Civil War, there lived in mountainous Mitchell County a kindly lady who had the rare gift of precognition. Judy Cook, the first of twenty-one children born to George Cook, a Baptist minister, resided with her family in a modest log cabin perched atop a mountain overlooking Dog Wood Flats in eastern Mitchell County. As the oldest child, Judy took care of most of her brothers and sisters in their formative years. As they grew, her siblings stood in awe of Judy's special ability to sense danger related to family members. When Judy, the beloved guardian angel of the Cook clan, had a premonition, everyone listened intently and heeded her words of warning.

But then came a chilly morning in November 1870. The trees had already been robbed of their beautiful autumn foliage, as winter was making a fast approach in the North Carolina mountains that year. Outside her cabin, Judy talked with her two favorite sisters, Jane and Harriet, as they prepared for a long journey on foot across the mountains to visit family in adjacent Carter County, Tennessee. Looming in the distance to the north was steep Roan Mountain. To reach their destination, Jane and Harriet would have to climb the towering peak, which stretched sixty-two hundred feet toward the heavens. Already, the sisters had postponed their trip after Harriet was stricken with milk sickness, a much-feared malady that was known to recur when its victim undertook extreme physical exertion. Now, there was no time to lose. If the visit were to be accomplished, the sisters would have to get under way immediately, for winter weather would render the rugged trail over the mountain impassable.

As Jane and Harriet prepared to take their leave, Judy suddenly had a premonition. Because what she foresaw was so terrible, she refused to reveal the details. However, she promptly urged her sisters to forgo the trip, as it would certainly result in death. Ordinarily, her pleas would have convinced them to cancel their plans, but neither lady wanted to again postpone a visit that had been planned for months. And after all, Harriet felt fine, looked healthy, and had apparently fully recovered from her recent illness.

Eschewing Judy's final desperate entreaties, the women exchanged farewell hugs and kisses with their elder sister and Harriet's two-year-old son. Then they were off. Judy held the little boy's hand tightly as they watched the women follow the path that snaked its way into the mountain wilderness. Nagging at Judy was the ominous feeling that her sisters were walking toward doom. And there was nothing she could do about it.

As they began their long walk, Jane and Harriet were confident in the knowledge that they had made the same trek over the mountains to Tennessee numerous times without incident. Before this day, however, they had always been in the company of men.

Their passage on the ancient trail first used by Indians was tedious and physically demanding, but the sisters arrived safely at the home of their kin in Rip Shin, Tennessee. Two days and nights of fellowship, fun, and rest followed.

Early on the clear, cold morning of the third day, the sisters struck out on the return trip. After several hours of brisk walking, Jane became alarmed because her sister looked pale and weak. By noon, it was evident that Harriet was suffering another bout of milk sickness. Her malaria-like fever was accompanied by vomiting and body tremors. Jane saw unfolding before her very eyes what her sister Judy had predicted just days before. Oh, how she wished she had heeded that premonition. Ahead of the sisters was the steep ascent of the tallest mountain separating them from the safety of home. And Harriet could hardly walk.

Their snail-like pace afforded Jane the opportunity to brood about Judy's haunting words. To make matters worse, there was no afternoon sun to warm the chilly air. Instead, ominous clouds clothed the skies and brisk, frigid winds whipped the slopes as Jane helped Harriet hobble along.

By nightfall, the wayfarers somehow reached the place at the summit of Roan Mountain that now bears Jane's name. Harriet, her body ravaged by illness, could go no farther and collapsed under a pine tree. Jane was completely helpless. The overcast sky enveloped the sisters in total darkness. There was no way to build a fire or provide light. The icy wind compounded their misery. Wild animals offered their menacing roars and cries.

Jane held her sister, who had lost consciousness, close to her body to provide warmth. The ground froze over the course of the seemingly endless night. Finally, the welcome rays of the sun greeted the pink dawn of the new day. Her body stiff from her cramped position, Jane staggered down the fog-shrouded mountain to the nearest cabin in the valley. There, she told the farmer of her terrible ordeal. Without hesitation, he made his way out into the cold morning, hitched his horses to a wagon, wrapped Jane in a warm blanket, and hastily proceeded up the mountain. Upon reaching the top, they found Harriet still unconscious but clinging to life. They gently lifted her onto a stack of warm bedding in the back of the buckboard.

Back at the Cook cabin, Judy, fearing that her premonition had been realized, wept openly and paced the floor as she awaited word from her overdue sisters. When family and friends attempted to comfort her, she implored them to assemble a search party for Jane and Harriet. But they reasoned that the sisters had decided to extend their stay.

Judy persisted to the point that a group of men set out from Dog Wood Flats to look for the missing women. Just as the search party turned the first curve, it met a wagon driven by a man recognized to be Charlie Young. Riding in the back was Jane, who was ministering to her prostrate sister. When the wagon pulled up to the Cook cabin, the men carried Harriet inside and carefully laid her in the bed of the sister who had foreseen the terrible tragedy. In but a short time, she was dead.

Today, hikers on the Appalachian Trail can reach the very spot where Jane and Harriet spent their harrowing night atop Roan Mountain. This site, one of the three prominent peaks of the mountain, memorializes the name of the survivor of that deadly premonition in 1870. It is called Jane's Bald.

THE ETERNAL FLAME

Whatever the scientists may say, if we take the supernatural out of life, we leave only the unnatural.

Amelia E. Barr

MOUNTAINOUS POLK COUNTY is home to one of the state's most unusual scientific phenomena—the thermal belt. On certain chilly nights, the temperature on the slopes of mountains in the county can be twenty degrees warmer than at the base. This temperate zone explains the success of the fruit-growing industry and the vacation and retirement resorts in the area.

Writer and scientific observer Silas McDowell first studied and documented the thermal belt in 1858. Yet how and where this climatological anomaly began continues to baffle scientists to this day. On the other hand, if you ask old-timers in Polk County, they can readily give you the details of the thermal belt's origin. As their story goes, the phenomenon was born of a fire started by Cherokee warriors during the colonial period. Local folks contend that the flames from that fire, never extinguished, continue to blaze to this very day at Stepp's Cove near the Polk County-Henderson County line.

When the first white settlers ventured into what is now Polk County in the eighteenth century, they entered a frontier that was the domain of the Cherokee Indians. As these incursions increased in number, there were numerous bloody clashes between the frontiersmen and the Indians. In an effort to quell the violence, Royal Governor William Tryon traveled to the area in 1767 to establish a boundary between the warring factions.

From the perspective of the James Step family, Governor Tryon's boundary did not achieve its intended result. Their plantation was located near Mill Spring, a town in central Polk County at the intersection of what are now NC 9 and NC 108. Anthony Allaire, a British lieutenant traveling in the company of the intrepid Scottish officer Patrick Ferguson during the week before the pivotal Revolutionary War battle at nearby Kings Mountain, gave a hint of the tragedy that befell the family in his diary entry of Friday, September 29, 1780: "We then, at that early hour, moved on three miles to one James Step's plantation and halted. This man has been very unfortunate in his family; his wife, who is a very decent woman, was caught by the Indians about twelve months past. They scalped her several times in the head, treated the infant she had in her arms in a most inhumane and savage manner. They mashed its head in such a manner that its recovery is truly astonishing; but what this poor unhappy woman seems most to regret is the loss of her oldest son, whom the savages took, and she now remains in a state of uncertainty, not having heard from since."

The attack described by Lieutenant Allaire took place after Mrs. Fannie Step and her children were captured at their plantation by the Indians while James Step was away. The captives were taken to a mountain cove near the western boundary of Polk

County. That cove now bears the family's name. While there, something spooked the Indians and caused them to launch the brutal attack on the defenseless family members.

After being scalped and savagely beaten with tomahawks, Fannie Step lay sprawled on the ground in a semiconscious condition. One of the Indians took little Polly, her infant daughter, and smashed her head into a tree. Revived by that terrible sight, Fannie attempted to fight back. In an instant, she was tied to a tree and forced to witness another horrible spectacle. Her eldest son, who had already been scalped, was tossed by the Indians onto a large pile of brush and wood, and a torch was placed to the pyre. Fannie fainted from shock, exposure, and loss of blood. Her last memory was the sight of her helpless child as the flames grew in intensity.

Little Polly Step never forgot the horrible attack on her family. Amazingly, she fully recovered from her head injury. As an adult, she took part in a fierce fight against marauding Indians at Point Lookout, a frontier stronghold near Stepp's Cove in eastern Henderson County. At the height of that battle, Polly fired the shots that mortally wounded the Cherokee chief. Excited by her feat, she spoke a line that survives as one of the most memorable from the early history of western North Carolina: "I've killed the Big Injun, damned if I ain't killed the Big Injun."

And what about the fire upon which Polly's older brother was placed at Stepp's Cove? According to Polk County tradition, the fire rages as hot as ever. In the years since the attack on the Step family, numerous hunters have happened upon the site of the great fire. Even in blinding snowstorms, they have found the place to be as warm as a fireplace.

Should you have occasion to vacation in the Polk County resort town of Tryon, remember that the unusually warm mountain air there is the product of a nearby phantom fire started centuries ago, when this land was the American frontier.

SHADOW OF A DOUBT

Beware of a man's shadow and a bee's sting.

Burmese proverb

IN 1971, historic preservationists lost a battle in Rutherfordton, the seat of Rutherford County, when the former county jail building, constructed around 1852, was razed to make room for a fast-food restaurant.

Ninety-one years earlier, Daniel Keith, a convicted murderer, lived out his last hours in the jail after losing the legal struggle to save his life. But Dan Keith, a self-acknowledged thief, liar, swindler, heavy drinker, and Lothario, may have been hanged for a crime he did not commit. Ever since he died at Gallows Field in Rutherfordton on December 11, 1880, his ghostly shadow has haunted the site of the old jail, as if to cast doubt on his guilt.

In late January 1880, big, burly Dan Keith, who stood six foot four and weighed 230 pounds, was taken into custody by N. E. Walker, the sheriff of Rutherford County, and charged with the rape and murder of Alice Ellis, a local black girl who was not yet a teenager. Dan's well-known reputation as a rogue was enough to make him a prime suspect. Born in 1848 in Pulaski County, Kentucky, to a poor dirt farmer, Dan was the youngest of eight children. His father died when the boy was just thirteen, which led him to rebel against his mother. A year later, he ran away from home and joined the Confederate army. His short stint ended with his desertion and flight to Indiana. As he awaited his execution eighteen years later, Dan reflected on his decision to desert: "It was one of those critical points in a man's life at which there is but an inch between the path to heaven and the road to hell."

His life of crime began with a series of petty thefts in Indiana. Then he returned to Kentucky, rejoined the Confederate army, and deserted once again. Over the next fifteen years, Dan used various aliases as he lied, cheated, and stole in Kentucky, Tennessee, and the Carolinas. For this crime spree, he spent but one year in prison. Meanwhile, he took—and abandoned—three wives.

In 1878, Dan settled with his fourth wife, a fifteen-year-old girl, in North Carolina. Not long thereafter, he perpetrated his most elaborate swindle. He took a large rock weighing sixty-eight pounds and rubbed it with brass until he could pass it off as gold to a number of gullible men. In the aftermath of the great hoax, Dan's many enemies vowed to exact revenge. It has been speculated that the death of Alice Ellis provided those adversaries with just the opportunity they needed.

On the afternoon of Wednesday, January 28, 1880, Alice's lifeless body was found in a wooded area of Rutherford County. Her head had been crushed with a heavy rock. Because of the brutal nature of the crime, authorities commenced an immediate search for the killer.

Acting on a tip that Dan had been observed near the little

girl's house earlier in the day, Sheriff Walker called at the Keith cabin around nine o'clock the night of the murder. According to the sheriff, Dan was sober. When questioned about the killing, he disavowed any knowledge of it. A search of the cabin, however, produced a shirt heavily stained with blood. Dan insisted that he had worn the garment while skinning rabbits. No one believed him, although numerous rabbit carcases were evident about the place.

When the sheriff arrested him, Dan did not resist. He left his home quietly, confident that he would be absolved of the crime. However, local sentiment was that the murder had been committed by a real brute. Given Dan's size and his notoriety, most folks reasoned that the guilty man had been taken into custody. Cognizant that some people wanted to summarily execute Dan, Sheriff Walker decided to transfer the accused to the Cleveland County Jail in Shelby, so as to thwart the plans of would-be lynch mobs.

Dan's trial was scheduled for the spring term of the Rutherford County Court. In anticipation of the trial, the defendant was returned to Rutherfordton and incarcerated in a cell on the south side of the county jail. On several occasions, the sheriff visited Dan in an attempt to gain a confession. Townspeople passing by the jail heard Dan's loud, angry voice during those confrontations. At length, Sheriff Walker realized the futility of his efforts when Dan glared at him and said, "I ain't killed nobody, and them what says I have will be snared in their own devilment."

When the day of the trial arrived, the crowd milling about the city streets had already convicted the defendant before a jury was impaneled. Inside the courtroom, the deck seemed to be stacked as well. Once the proceedings got under way, fifteen witnesses were called to the stand to testify against Dan. Not one of them had seen the crime committed. Some of the testimony was obviously fabricated. All of the evidence presented against the defendant was circumstantial.

Then it was Dan's turn. When he took the stand, his booming voice resonated up and down the halls of the courthouse and could even be heard by people standing on the street outside the building. Attired in a homemade bright green shirt, he tried to convince the jurors he was an innocent man. Unfortunately for the defendant, the most compelling evidence on his behalf was ruled inadmissable by the court. A man from nearby McDowell County had escaped from jail in recent days. That fugitive had been awaiting execution for the same rape and murder for which Dan Keith was now being tried.

In his closing argument, the prosecutor did his best to inflame the passions of the jurors. Hoping to arouse their fear and anger, he thundered, "What innocent little child gathering the dewy blossoms of spring, what flower of Southern womanhood, nay, what one of us can be safe from attack by such a monster as this creature before us? Ah, gentlemen, a mad beast deserves but one fate. In the name of that young life which he so mercilessly struck down, I implore you to find Daniel Keith guilty of murder!"

It took the jurors but a half-hour to render a verdict. Upon their return to the courtroom, Dan was ordered to stand as the decision was announced. To the surprise of no one save the defendant, the jury proclaimed, "We find the prisoner at the bar, Daniel Keith, guilty of murder." Thunderous applause and shouts of approval threatened to disrupt the courtroom decorum.

After gaveling the spectators to order, the judge gave Dan an opportunity to make a statement before the sentence was imposed. As he stared into the eyes of the jurors and the witnesses who had testified against him, the defendant exhibited no remorse. Indeed, he boldly intimated a threat: "Those who say I kilt anybody are liars. And each of you will be hainted every day for the rest of your life. Then the devil will have ye."

When Dan finished, the judge pronounced the sentence that the community wanted and expected: "Then it is the judgment of this court that the prisoner, Daniel Keith, be remanded to the Common Jail of the county and there remain until the 11th day of December next, and that he then be taken by the said N. E. Walker, High Sheriff, as aforesaid, from the jail to the place of execution between the hours of ten o'clock in the morning and two o'clock in the afternoon, and there he be hanged by the neck until he be dead, dead, dead."

An appeal to the North Carolina Supreme Court resulted in the affirmation of the verdict and death sentence.

Dan awaited his fate in his cell on the south wall of the Rutherford County Jail. Less than a month before his execution, he purportedly made a confession. However, the vocabulary, sentence structure, and grammar in that "confession"—which was subsequently published and sold by his attorney—hinted that the alleged admission of guilt may have been the product of the lawyer, rather than the client. From the outset of the case, Dan had done little to foster a healthy attorney-client relationship. To induce his lawyer to handle the matter, Dan had conned him into believing he had hidden the money from a Kentucky bank robbery in McDowell County. Dan went so far as to draw a fake map. After three or four fruitless searches, the attorney realized he had been duped.

On the day before the execution, wagonloads of people began to pour into Rutherfordton. It was apparent that Dan would receive no reprieve.

Early the next morning, Sheriff Walker visited the condemned man in his cell. Resolute as ever, Dan declared, "The soul of an innocent man don't rest, sheriff. Nor can mine 'til I prove to you and them on the jury that I'm going blameless to the gallows."

Around noon, Dan boarded the death cart. As it rolled down the city streets, he sat between the sheriff and a deputy, seemingly oblivious to the jeers of the persons who had braved the December cold to witness the macabre spectacle. When the parade of death reached Gallows Field, Dan calmly annunciated his innocence one last time just before the noose was placed around his neck. Then, in a sarcastic tone, he urged Sheriff Walker to "keep a cool head and not become excited."

At one o'clock, the door on the hanging platform dropped, the rope snapped Dan's thick neck, and, as the *Charlotte Observer* put it, "the world [was] rid of a monster." Within hours, the large crowd dissipated. It was all over. Or was it?

Just days after the execution, folks in Rutherfordton began to notice something peculiar about the exterior of the county jail. On the south wall was an ominous shadow in the likeness of a hanged man. Townspeople familiar with Dan's haunting threats feared that the executed man was making good on them.

Initially, Sheriff Walker thought otherwise. He was of the opinion that the shadow was nothing more than a tasteless prank. But it was still there the next day, and the next, and the next. As word spread, large numbers of curious people made their way to Rutherfordton to see the phenomenon for themselves. Embarrassed by a situation that was quickly getting out of control, the sheriff attempted in vain to scrub the shadow off the wall. Then he ordered the wall to be painted. Within days, the hanged man returned. Nothing would make it go away. Even in the dark of night, it was clearly visible.

After the county jail was transferred to another location, the old building was converted into a private home. Some people speculated that the shadow might disappear, but it remained as distinct as ever. Plagued by the constant stream of visitors intrigued by the south wall, the owner planted ivy to cover the shadow.

In 1949, the structure was transformed into an office building. During the renovation, several coats of paint were applied to the exterior. Finally, it appeared that Dan's haunting shadow was no more. Perhaps his spirit had given up.

There seemed little doubt that Dan's vow to haunt his accusers was at an end when the old jail building was acquired and demolished by the Catawba County Valley Investment Company in 1971. The company promptly constructed one of its Burger House restaurants on the site. But the business never proved successful. That Burger House and all the other franchise stores closed permanently within a two-year period.

No one attributed the business collapse to Dan's threat until other ventures housed in the new building failed. Even a combination video store-pizza shop-ice cream parlor—aptly named Daniel Keith's Video—could not make it at the site of the old jail.

And then the shadow reappeared when the new building housed another restaurant. Wait staff carrying out the trash after hours were often spooked by the shadow. When closing the establishment each night, the manager would lock the building after making sure everything was in order. But the next morning would invariably find a table set for one in the corner of the place.

For whatever reason, no business has been able to endure at the site since the old jail was torn down. A nationally franchised pizza restaurant currently resides there. There are those who say that Dan's shadow is still visible on the wall some nights. Will his curse spell doom for the existing business? Considering that old Dan has made good on his threat ever since 1880, some locals say it will happen beyond a shadow of a doubt.

GHOST HOUND OF A GHOST TOWN

Shadowy forms, and ghosts and sleepy things . . .

Philip Frenau

HISTORIC ROCKFORD, the former seat of Surry County, is little more than a shadow of its former self. Established in 1791 on the banks of the Yadkin River, this town suffered two significant blows within a seventy-five-year period that diminished its importance and sent it into a tailspin from which it has never recovered. When Surry County was divided in 1850, the county seat was moved to Dobson. And in 1916, the rain-gorged Yadkin flooded Rockford, destroying roads, bridges, and the railroad. Thereafter, the population began a steady decline. Businesses and homes were abandoned. Today, though Rockford is a virtual ghost town, there abides here a supernatural presence, a ghost dog, dating from the time when the river-front village enjoyed a measure of prominence.

As it makes its way down the hill to the old White Rock

Ford on the Yadkin, the once-bustling main street of Rockford passes an impressive assemblage of structures listed on the National Register of Historic Places. Included in the collection are the former Surry County Courthouse (1830); the fire-damaged Grand Hotel (c. 1796); a tobacco factory (c. 1848); the Masonic Hall (c. 1797); the former Methodist church (1913), adorned with a magnificent fresco painted by Tony Griffin, the brother-in-law of noted artist Ben Long; the York Tavern (1837); and the Rockford General Store (1921), one of the few signs of life remaining here. In its heyday, Rockford played host to a number of distinguished visitors, including James K. Polk, Aaron Burr, and Dorothea Dix. In his days as a young attorney, Andrew Jackson had his legal practice here for a time. Vacant, long-abandoned buildings are now the only reminders of the presence of such noteworthy people. On stormy nights, however, the bloodcurdling howl of a phantom dog can yet be heard.

The ghostly sound is said to emanate from the hill above the old graveyard in Rockford. After it was first heard, townspeople refused to go anywhere near the cemetery once the sun went down. Local folks have always believed that the howl is that of the ghost of a dog that belonged to an old man known as Still Face. He was so named by the children of Rockford because his face never countenanced a smile. Still Face lived with Hettie, his spinster sister, down along the river in a ramshackle cabin. He spent his days hunting with his devoted hound dog. Other than his rather sour disposition, the residents of Rockford had no reason to dislike Still Face. He was a loner and bothered no one.

When Hettie fell seriously ill one day, Still Face's life took a sad turn. She lasted but a week, and her death devastated her brother. Sympathetic residents of the town came to comfort the old man and to assist with the funeral arrangements. After the services, no one ever saw Still Face alive again—except for maybe Charlie Wilson.

About a week after the funeral, Charlie, the local mail carrier, was driving his two horse wagon along the road near the graveyard where Hettie had been laid to rest. A powerful thunderstorm had rendered the roads virtually impassable, causing Charley to fall behind on his route. Anxious to finish his rounds before the weather and road conditions grew any worse, he goaded the horses as lightning flashed and thunder boomed around him.

When the wagon lumbered past the graveyard, he heard an ominous moan amid the tombstones. Charlie glanced in the direction of the sound just as a wicked bolt of lightning illuminated the cemetery. What he saw chilled his bones. There, atop one of the gravestones, was either a man or a ghost! Sitting nearby was a rain-drenched dog.

Charlie urged his team to speed away from the spooky sight. When the mail wagon reached the store in Rockford, old man Gink, the owner, was skeptical about the story the highly agitated Charlie related. Gink said that most likely it was nothing more than a tree blowing in the heavy wind. Neither Gink nor Charlie even considered that the figures could have been Still Face and his hound at Hettie's grave.

Three uneventful days passed. Then, about midnight of the third day, most folks in the town were awakened by the plaintive yelping of a dog. The sound came from the direction of Still Face's cabin. All night long, the melancholy wail sounded throughout the community. Concerned that something was amiss, neighbors made their way to the cabin at first light. They found the lifeless body of Still Face in his bed.

As a result of the strange occurrences around Rockford over the previous few days, the citizens refused to allow Still Face to be laid to rest in the graveyard, fearing he would contaminate the souls of their loved ones buried there. Accordingly, the old man's corpse was to be transported to Yadkinville for interment.

About four o'clock in the afternoon, the wooden coffin bearing Still Face's body was loaded onto Charlie Wilson's mail wagon. Charlie realized that it would be dark before he reached Yadkinville, and he was feeling very uneasy about his unusual cargo. Concern was evident on his face when he begged some of the men assembled at the store in Rockford to accompany him. But no one was willing to take a nighttime ride with the body of old Still Face. Finally, Charlie drove off alone. One of his friends called out in jest, "The mail must go through, Charlie, so don't slack yer duty."

Four miles into the journey, the skies grew black as another storm covered the Yadkin Valley. Charlie looked to the flickering kerosene lantern at the side of the wagon for reassurance as he passed through a forbidding wilderness area. Then, from the back of the wagon, he heard it—a tapping sound that grew in intensity. Charlie was paralyzed with fear. Without looking, he knew that the racket was coming from the coffin. And his nightmare was only beginning. With a hideous shriek and the crack of splintering wood, the lid of the coffin popped off.

In an instant, Charlie drew his team to a halt, jumped from the wagon, and ran as hard as he could to the store at Rockford. Those who saw the rain-soaked man when he arrived said that he was as white as a sheet. Some disbelieved the words coming from his mouth, but others knew the truth when they looked into his terror-filled eyes.

The following day, John Borden, who lived on an island in the Yadkin, spotted Charlie's wagon, the horses still hitched to it, beside the river. Some men from Rockford made their way to fetch the wagon. They found the casket with its top split open, just as Charlie had described it. But the coffin was empty!

No one ever found the body of Still Face. Memories of the horrifying ordeal haunted Charlie Wilson for the rest of his days.

He gave up his mail route, became ill, and died within a few years.

Should you care to see Rockford as it completes its evolution into a true ghost town, it is located six miles north of Yadkinville on SR 1221 (Rockford Road). A daytime drive through this ancient place offers a fascinating look into its historic past. But beware of visiting after dark. The old cemetery has terrified people for years. On stormy nights, there's a constant sad howl of a ghost hound still searching for its master.

SPIRIT OF THE CHEROKEES

And the mist upon the hill,
Shadowy, shadowy, yet unbroken,
Is a symbol and a token
How it hangs upon the trees
A mystery of mysteries!

Edgar Allen Poe

MAJESTIC IN APPEARANCE and enormous in size, Fontana Lake was created in the 1940s when the Tennessee Valley Authority constructed a dam on the Little Tennessee River. Thirty miles long, the lake sprawls over 10,530 acres in the western and central portions of Swain County and the northern part of Graham County. Since the lake's completion in 1945, its waters—which reach a depth of 480 feet—have covered many historic sites of the Cherokee Indians. Claimed by the lake were the graves of Tsali, two of his sons, and his brother-in-law.

To this day, the memory of Tsali burns brightly in the hearts and minds of the Cherokee people as one of their greatest heroes. Had it not been for his courage and sacrifice, the Cherokees would have vanished from the North Carolina landscape long ago. And even though his final resting place was flooded, Tsali's presence lingers here, for his ghost is said to walk the ancient trails and ridges of the Great Smoky Mountains in Swain County.

Tsali emerged as a champion of the Cherokee Nation during the forced relocation of the Indians of the western Carolinas, eastern Tennessee, northern Georgia, and northeastern Alabama. Indeed, he was a principal player in the sad chapter of American history that had its beginnings in the wake of the American Revolution. For a thirty-year period beginning in 1785, the Cherokee Nation in the eastern United States maintained a tenuous grip on its homeland as a result of ceaseless incursions by white settlers. Its fate was sealed in 1815 when a little Indian lad discovered a piece of yellow metal while playing in a creek in northern Georgia. After his mother washed and polished it, she made the mistake of showing it to a group of white men. Suddenly, a cry was heard far and wide: "There's gold on the Cherokee land!"

Over the next twenty-three years, the federal government made various attempts to convince the Cherokees to move to the western territories of the United States. During that time, a number of highly respected members of Congress, including Henry Clay, Davy Crockett, and Daniel Webster, served as eloquent advocates for the Indians. Despite their efforts, numerous broken treaties and the indiscriminate slaughter of Indian men, women, and children culminated in the infamous Trail of Tears in 1838. The president and Congress issued a decree that year: The Cherokees were to be rounded up by military forces and moved across the Mississippi River to their new home in the West.

That May, General Winfield Scott and his seven-thousand-man army arrived in the North Carolina mountains to begin their onerous task of removing the Cherokees. From the outset, General Scott was anxious to move the project forward with all due speed. His soldiers were given a concise directive: "The emigration must begin before the full moon."

Without delay, the American troops went to work building the forts and stockades that were to serve as detention centers until the first wave of Cherokees could be sent west. Then came the roundup. Indian families were captured and taken prisoner while they worked and played—in the fields, in their homes, and in the forests. More than seventeen thousand men, women, and children were treated little better than cattle in the massive campaign. One of Scott's soldiers, a Georgian who would later fight with the Confederate army during the Civil War, wrote of his military service against the Cherokees: "I fought through the Civil War and have seen men shot to pieces and slaughtered by the thousands, but the Cherokee removal was the cruelest work I ever knew."

Ultimately, most of the Cherokees were forced to embark upon the great westward migration. Over the course of the heartbreaking journey, four thousand Indians of all ages died from torture and exposure to the elements. Their bones were scattered about the route of the Trail of Tears. But there was one stalwart Cherokee who was determined to remain in his homeland. As soon as Tsali received word of the orders to drive his people from the Great Smokies, he resolved to defy the authorities.

It was at the time of corn planting that American troops descended upon the Oconaluftee Valley, where they surprised Tsali and his family. The captured Indians were put on a forced march toward Fort Bushnell, the site of which is now covered by Fontana Lake. During the journey on the steep and physically demanding route, Tsali's wife stumbled. When a soldier prodded her with his bayonet to quicken her pace, Tsali was overcome with rage. Speaking in Cherokee, he proposed an escape plan to his three sons and his brother-in-law. He concluded with these words: "We shall all break free, but whatever happens, there must be no bloodshed."

At a place where the trail curved, the Indian men sprang on the soldiers and threw them to the ground, thereby allowing the women and children to flee into the forest. In the melee, a soldier's gun accidentally discharged and killed one of General Scott's men. Amid the confusion, Tsali was able to escape with his family to the relative safety of a cave on Clingman's Dome. Other Cherokees who managed to elude capture similarly went into hiding in the hills of the Great Smokies.

Those Indians presented a vexing problem for General Scott: they were almost impossible to find. To remedy the situation, the general turned to William Holland Thomas, a highly regarded white chief who was a close friend of Yonaguska, a noted Cherokee chief. Scott gave Thomas explicit instructions: "Find Tsali. Tell him if he will surrender and pay the penalty for the death of the soldier, I will intercede for the fugitives and have the government grant them permission to live in the Great Smokies. If he refuses, I'll turn my soldiers loose to hunt down each of them."

When Thomas found Tsali, he relayed the ultimatum. Tsali received his words with mixed emotions. He was thrilled with the guarantee that his people would be allowed to remain in their beloved hills, but he was bitter because his wife had starved to death during the exile. And now, he would be forced to give up his own life. Yet his reply to Thomas was simple and direct: "I will come and my family with me."

Tsali, his sons, and his brother-in-law set out for Fort Bushnell at the time of the harvest moon in October. Upon their arrival, General Scott ordered a detachment of Cherokee prisoners to form a firing squad. Tsali, his two eldest sons, and his brother-in-law were then shot to death by the Indian marksmen. Scott reasoned that this unusual execution would impress upon the Cherokees the futility of further resistance. On the other hand, General Scott displayed a measure of compassion in two of his decisions. He spared Tsali's fourteen-year-old son, Wesituni, from the firing squad—"because we do not shoot children," in his words. And he agreed to honor his promise that the Cherokees still present in their native land could remain.

Some say the ghost of Tsali soon made its appearance to ensure that General Scott and the federal government did not renege on the agreement. Just when the ghost was first encountered is uncertain, but in the waning days of the Civil War, some of General George Stoneman's Yankee raiders reported eerie incidents while on duty in the mountains. On a number of occasions, they sighted the apparition of a Cherokee brave wearing a cloth turban, a hunting shirt, and buckskin trousers. He carried a long rifle. All attempts to shoot the Indian were unsuccessful. "Our bullets went straight through him," the soldiers noted.

More visitors come to Great Smoky Mountains National Park than any other recreational area under the auspices of the National Park Service. Because most patrons travel to the park to partake of the splendid mountain scenery, they come during daylight hours. By the time the sun sets below the mirror-like waters of Fontana Lake, the majority of visitors have come and gone. Remaining behind, however, is the oldest permanent resident of the park—the ghost of Tsali.

Over the years, many eyewitnesses have observed this spectre. It watches over the people who continue to reside at the Cherokee Indian Reservation as a result of Tsali's sacrifice, and it patiently waits for the return of the people who were driven away.

Should you happen to be driving through the mountains of

Swain County on an October night when a harvest moon illu-
minates the peaks and ridges, keep a sharp eye for the ghostly
figure of a lonely old Indian. But don't blink, because the ghost
vanishes quickly. It is elusive, and for good reason. Tsali and his
people were once hunted down and captured like wild animals.
He gave his life for his homeland. But his ghost, which represents the enduring spirit of the Cherokee people, lives on as a
haunting reminder of the horror of man's inhumanity to man.

WHEN COINCIDENCE MARRIED FATE

It is a mistake to confound strangeness with mystery.

Sir Arthur Conan Doyle

FATE AND COINCIDENCE play a role in the life of every person. But the story of Julia Nathalie Forsythe defies explanation.

Most visitors to the historic Gillespie Cemetery in Brevard, the seat of Transylvania County, stroll past Julia's grave without paying attention to it. But if they were to give the marker close scrutiny, they would note a chain of dates that lies somewhere between coincidence and the supernatural.

Julia came into the world on Monday, May 14, 1860. There was nothing unusual about the fine spring day on which she was born. At that time, James Buchanan was president of the United States and John W. Ellis of Salisbury was governor of North Carolina. The Civil War was almost a year away. Yet the day and date on which Julia was born put into motion one of the oddest sets of events ever recorded in the history of the state.

During her first sixteen years, Julia lived a normal life. She grew into a beautiful teenager who caught the eye of many young men. When her favorite suitor proposed to her, Julia accepted.

The couple selected as their big day the bride's seventeenth birthday—May 14, 1877. Most folks said it was mere coincidence that the wedding day fell on a Monday, the same day as Julia's birth.

By all accounts, the marriage was a happy one. There was nothing unusual about it other than the fact that Julia lived precisely one-half of her married life in the nineteenth century and the other half in the twentieth.

Julia Nathalie Forsythe died in 1923. When the craftsman charged with the task of chiseling the dates on her tombstone commenced his work, his reaction was a mixture of wonder and astonishment—much like cemetery visitors in modern times. Her marker displays the incredible fact that she was born, married, and died on the same day and date of the same month:

Julia Nathalie Forsythe
Born Monday, May 14, 1860
Married Monday, May 14, 1877
Died Monday, May 14, 1923

THE BUGLER

O day and night, but this is wondrous strange!

William Shakespeare

IN A REMOTE MOUNTAINOUS area located between Laurel Creek Road (SR 1123) and Rominger Road in southwestern Watauga County, there is a rock ledge set on a lofty ridge that towers high above the surrounding valleys. During the first half of the nineteenth century, this unusual rock outcrop gained the name it bears today—Bugle Rock. According to legend, the ghost of a pre-Civil War bugler plays his horn from the ledge to this very day.

Although this part of Watauga County remains sparsely populated, far fewer people lived in the coves and on the mountainsides in the 1830s and 1840s. Among the area residents of that time were Andy Hicks and his family, who resided on a ridge near Bugle Rock. Andy was an accomplished bugler who was well respected by his scattered neighbors. When someone needed medical attention or when the folks living on the peaks and in the valleys needed to be summoned, Andy would take his prized musical instrument to Bugle Rock, where he would blow loud and long. In response to Andy's clarion call, neighbors from far and wide would assemble at the Hicks cabin.

Without question, Andy's biggest admirer was his mother, who loved to sit and listen as he played hymns on his bugle. On the day she died in 1842, Andy came home and promptly walked to his perch atop Bugle Rock. And then the valleys and coves were filled with the sweet sounds that his mother had loved to hear him produce from his shiny brass instrument.

Mrs. Hicks was laid to rest in a small family cemetery near Bugle Rock in an area that is still known as Sammy Fields. For the rest of his life, Andy returned to his favorite spot to serenade his mother's grave.

Over the many years since Andy's death, much of the wilderness surrounding Bugle Rock has been transformed into pasture land and crop fields. In the middle of one such clearing is the white-pine thicket that hides the grave of Andy's mother. Her headstone, crafted from soapstone, bears crudely carved inscriptions of her name, date of birth, and date of death. Several other graves marked only by fieldstones are also located in the badly overgrown cemetery.

After Andy joined his mother in death, Bugle Rock lost its music. Or did it? Some residents of the nearby hills and vales claim that Andy's ghost makes its way to the rock ledge on occasion to serenade his beloved mother. Motorists traveling this isolated part of Watauga County might do well to listen for the melodious music that comes from the phantom horn of Andy Hicks atop Bugle Rock.

MOUNTAIN OF THE MACABRE

As after sunset fadeth in the west;
Which by and by black night doth take away,
Death's second self, that seals up all in rest . . .

William Shakespeare

LOCATED in the northwestern part of the state, mountainous Wilkes County has been the source of many intriguing legends since it was created by the legislature in 1778, while North Carolina was fighting for American independence. Throughout much of the history of Wilkes, the dense forests growing on its peaks, in its isolated coves, and along its numerous streams have provided both a workplace for woodsmen and protection for the covert activities of moonshiners.

One prominent waterway is Stony Fork Creek, a tributary of the Yadkin River that rises in eastern Watauga County and flows southeast into western Wilkes County. Just east of this creek, US 421 passes Laurel Spur Ridge, which serves as a natural boundary between Wilkes and Watauga. Despite its picturesque beauty, this mountain remains a haunted place as a result of a heinous event that occurred here in the nineteenth century.

The names of the principal players in the gruesome drama that unfolded in a mountainside home so long ago have been lost to history. One deep, dark evening around midnight, the man of the house, who was quite fond of the liquor produced in these hills, stormed into the modest cabin in an inebriated condition. His loud entry awakened his wife, and a heated argument ensued. The mixture of rage and moonshine produced a violent outburst. The husband savagely attacked and killed his wife. Anxious to dispose of the body, he carried it outside into the early-morning darkness and threw it into an abandoned well not far from the cabin.

Upon his return to the house, the man was irritated by the cries of his small child, who had been startled from its slumber by the fight. Taking the child in his arms, he walked back to the old well, where he proceeded to compound his ghastly crime. Without hesitation, he dropped the screaming youngster into the dark depths of the hole. Over the next few days, the poor child died a slow, painful death near the cadaver of its murdered mother.

Although the man was never brought to justice, he could not bear to reside in the cabin on Laurel Spur Ridge for long. For many years thereafter, the structure stood abandoned. Among the mountain folk, it gained a reputation as a "hainted" place.

Finally, two loggers who were brothers proved either brave or adventurous enough to take up residence in the weather-beaten shack. Ab and Joe Johnson operated a sawmill nearby. The cabin seemed a most convenient place for them to sleep and take their meals. To shelter their work animals, they fabricated a crude stable from the lumber they harvested on the mountain. That stable stood near the cabin.

The brothers knew the details of the horrid events that had transpired on the property and the sinister tales connected with the place. Consequently, they refused to sleep in the bedroom where the murder had occurred. Unwilling to chance an encounter with the ghosts rumored to haunt the room, the Johnsons made sure that its door was locked tight every night before they retired.

For two or three months, all went well. But then came a night of sheer terror the likes of which few humans have ever lived to describe. It started about midnight when a loud banging sound emanating from the bedroom of death caused Joe, the more daring of the brothers, to sit straight up in bed. His fear intensified when the locked door suddenly flew open. Desperately needing the companionship of his brother, he called out, "Ab, wake up!"

Aroused from a deep sleep, Ab squinted in the darkness and responded, "What is it, Joe? What ails ye?"

Scared out of his wits, Joe was all too happy to have company in his time of horror. In a voice that was little more than a whisper, he implored, "Listen! Listen at that noise in yonder."

Both men were rugged outdoorsmen wise in the ways of the mountain wilderness. Yet at this moment, they were too afraid to move. In the darkness of that mountain night, they listened intently to the footsteps on the creaky wooden floor of the bedroom of death. Then they distinctly heard the voice of a man uttering angry profanities. A bloodcurdling scream from a female soon followed. Almost as quickly as the terrifying shriek began, it ended. And then Joe and Ab detected the sounds of a whimpering child.

When the cabin was once again silent, Ab mustered the courage to say, "Land of Goshen! What is it, Joe?"

Joe pondered the situation without comment for a few seconds. He then attempted to provide a pragmatic explanation: "Jest the steers up at the stable. Must be a dang wildcat messin' round up there."

With that, Joe slowly and cautiously climbed out of bed. Clothed in nothing more than his underwear, he pulled on his boots and picked up his shotgun. Ab followed suit and made his way out of the cabin close behind Joe. Outside, the brothers encountered the darkest night that either had ever beheld.

As they proceeded toward the stable, they happened upon the old well, now covered with rotting planks. Ab stopped in his tracks when he heard an agonizing cry coming from the hole. Unable to mask his fear, he mumbled, "Did ye hear that, Joe?"

Like his brother, Joe was aghast. The sounds rising from the dank, dark pit were the cries of a child suffering from pain and fright.

Neither brother was brave enough to examine the well to ascertain the origin of the eerie sounds. Instead, the almost naked men fled into the wilderness. They finally reached the safety of a distant neighbor's home three hours later.

Ab and Joe Johnson never returned to the site of their night of horror. As far as anyone knows, no one was ever willing to spend another night in the house, which thereafter fell into ruin. It was reclaimed by nature and no longer stands.

Hikers who explore the pristine wilderness of Laurel Spur Ridge are strongly advised to avoid any abandoned wells they might find. Not only do these old wells pose safety hazards, but one in particular offers up the ghostly whimpers of a child who continues to haunt this mountain of the macabre.

OF CREATURES UNKNOWN

We are prodding, challenging, seeking contradictions or small, persistent residual errors, proposing alternative explanations, encouraging heresy. We give our highest rewards to those who convincingly disprove established beliefs.

Carl Sagan

CRYPTOZOOLOGY is the study and investigation of animal species that have not yet been proven to exist through the scientific method, even though empirical evidence shows otherwise. On record are numerous eyewitness accounts of such legendary creatures as giant sea serpents, the Abominable Snowman, and the Loch Ness Monster. However, because no specimen of any of these mysterious animals has been produced for scientific examination, they do not officially exist.

In North America, the most famous cryptid is Bigfoot, also known as Sasquatch. Coined in the late 1950s, the name Bigfoot is applied to large, hairy, humanoid creatures that have been spotted in the wilds of Canada and many states, including North Carolina, for centuries. From the numerous reported human encounters with the mysterious animal, a good composite description of it has emerged: an adult Bigfoot ranges in height from six to ten feet and weighs more than a human; short to medium-length straight, dark hair covers its body except for its face, which is flat and dark; and its arms, equipped with hands, extend to the mid-thigh. Most of the creatures have been observed walking or standing on their two feet, much in the manner of humans.

Despite having many physical features similar to those of humans, the Bigfoot has exhibited some characteristics that proved terrifying or revolting to witnesses. Reports indicate that the creature can unleash a bloodcurdling howl or scream. Equally horrifying are the glowing eyes of red, green, or yellow. But perhaps the most onerous thing reported about the Bigfoot is its foul odor. Various words have been used to describe the unforgettable smell: *powerful, nauseating, sickening, rancid, overpowering, vile, putrid*. Witnesses have reported that it smelled like rotten eggs, dead fish, or an outhouse. So terrible is the scent that the animal is alternately known in some places as the Skunk Ape.

Although the majority of recent sightings have occurred in the Pacific Northwest, credible accounts of encounters with Bigfoot or the discovery of its tracks have been received from all parts of North Carolina over the past half-century. Because of the vast areas of rugged wilderness that still exist in the mountains, it is easy to understand why western North Carolina has been a popular place for reports of Bigfoot activity. A longstanding tradition of Swain, Jackson, and Haywood Counties tells of the Boojum, the "Bigfoot of the Balsams." This legendary half-human, half-ape creature allegedly roamed the Great Smokies in the nineteenth century.

One of the first published articles concerning a Bigfoot-like animal in North America appeared in the *Boston Gazette* in July 1793. This account told of a creature that had been observed in the Bald Mountains, a range shared by Yancey County and several other counties in North Carolina and Tennessee. The article contained a detailed description of the beast: "This animal is between twelve and fifteen feet high, and in shape resembling a human being, except the head, which is equal in proportion to its body and drawn in somewhat like a terrapin; its feet are . . . about two feet long, and hairy, which is of a dark dun colour; its eyes are exceedingly large."

In almost every respect, the newspaper description of the Bigfoot sighted in the eighteenth century is an uncanny match for that of the creatures observed in the Tar Heel State and other places in the late twentieth century. But there was one sinister characteristic in the early account not often found in more recent reports: "These animals are bold and have lately attempted to kill several persons—in which attempt some of them have been shot. Their principal resort is on the Bald Mountain, where they lay in wait for travelers." In modern times, there have been no credible reports of Bigfoot attacks on humans in North Carolina.

Does such a creature still live in the North Carolina mountains? If two accounts from the Yancey County area are accurate, then it appears that such a cryptid indeed exists.

One night in mid-March 1988, a group of friends drove to the top of Mount Mitchell in their four-wheel-drive vehicle. Ascending the 6,684-foot peak, the tallest east of the Mississippi River, was treacherous because the heavy snowfalls of early March had left deep drifts along the road, which was officially closed during the winter. After a brief sojourn at the summit, the men began the trip down the mountain. Approximately a half-mile into the descent, their headlights illuminated a steep snowbank as the vehicle made a sharp turn. There in the snow were a number of large, deep impressions that led up the bank and into the mountain forest. Because the night was very dark, the men could not study the strange marks closely. They resumed their descent after agreeing to return to the site in daylight.

The men came back the next day to examine the tracks and the surrounding landscape. They measured the snow depth at eighteen inches, and the tracks extended all the way to the bottom. Faint outlines in the two tracks closest to the road appeared to be toe marks—but not those of a bear, since there were no claw marks. Shocked by what they saw, the friends concluded that the impressions had been made by a bipedal animal.

To investigate the tracks leading up the steep bank, the tallest of the men—an athletic fellow who stood six foot two—climbed the incline in eight strides. But whatever left the footprints had accomplished the same climb in just two steps. Above the slope, the creature had walked over a fallen tree limb three feet above the ground without altering its stride. After taking into account some melting of the snow at the impressions, the men calculated the footprints to be fourteen inches long and seven inches wide.

Although the Mount Mitchell party did not see the creature that left the unusual prints, two men traveling to Virginia through the same area just after midnight on November 15, 1975, came face to face with a beast they believed to be a Bigfoot. Their headlights revealed a large thing sitting in the middle of the road about a quarter-mile ahead. Slowly, they drove to within ten feet of the animal. Suddenly, it stood up on two feet!

The eyewitness who filed the report was an experienced hunter who had roamed this portion of the North Carolina mountains for many years. During his adventures, he had become familiar with virtually every species of wildlife that lived in these hills. But never had he seen anything like this. He knew what bear looked like, and this was no bear. Staring at the thing in utter disbelief, the fellow was mortified with fear.

Before the creature walked away into the woods, the two

occupants of the vehicle got a good view of it in the headlights. Covered in black fur, it possessed broad shoulders and arms that stretched to its knees. They estimated its weight to be as much as five hundred pounds and its height to be eight feet. Because the headlights were very bright in the mountain darkness, the animal turned its head away, thus depriving the men of a glimpse of its face. For a brief moment, they were afraid that it was going to jump on the hood of their car. Instead, it bounded away, maintaining a stooped position. It needed only four steps to cover twenty-five yards.

About the time of this sighting, residents of the area reported unusual animal sounds, strange smells, and spooked pets.

Scarcely a week goes by without a supermarket tabloid offering a front-page story about Bigfoot. These stories do little to lend credibility to the belief that this creature actually exists. Accordingly, until a live specimen is captured or a legitimate corpse is produced, Bigfoot will remain a cryptid. Be that as it may, a human-like creature with enormous feet has been sighted in the mountains of North Carolina from the earliest history of the United States. Could it be anything but a Bigfoot?